Trixie knew she couldn't hide from the truth forever.

Even though no one, absolutely no one, in Dallas knew about the baby, Trixie knew in her heart, knew in her soul, that somewhere out there she had a child.

It was her great secret, her great burden to bear. She had yet to forgive herself for her one youthful indiscretion, or for allowing those around her to force her to send her child away.

Sometimes she lay awake at night, asking God to help her bear the sorrow of her secret.

Did God ever hear her pleas? Could she ever be whole again?

Tomorrow she would face her past. Face the man she had loved so fiercely.

And Trixie desperately wished she could turn back time....

LENORA WORTH

grew up in a small Georgia town and decided in the fourth grade that she wanted to write. But first, she married her high school sweetheart, then moved to Atlanta, Georgia. Taking care of their baby daughter at home while her husband worked at night, Lenora discovered the world of romance novels and knew that's what she wanted to write. And so she began.

A few years later, the family settled in Shreveport, Louisiana, where Lenora continued to write while working as a marketing assistant. After the birth of her second child, a boy, she decided to pursue full time her dream of writing. In 1993, Lenora's hard work and determination finally paid off with that first sale.

"I never gave up, and I believe my faith in God helped get me through the rough times when I doubted myself," Lenora says. "Each time I start a new book, I say a prayer, asking God to give me the strength and direction to put the words to paper. That's why I'm so thrilled to be a part of Steeple Hill's Love Inspired line, where I get to combine my faith in God with my love of romance. It's the best combination."

Logan's Child
Lenora Worth

™ *Love Inspired*™

Published by Steeple Hill Books™

STEEPLE HILL BOOKS

Steeple
Hill™

ISBN 0-373-87026-4

LOGAN'S CHILD

Printed in U.S.A.

Those who sow in tears
shall reap in joy.
He who continually goes forth weeping,
bearing seed for sowing,
shall doubtless come again with rejoicing,
bringing his sheaves with him.
—Psalm 126:5-6

For his anger endureth but a moment;
in his favor is life:
weeping may endure for a night,
but joy cometh in the morning.
—Psalm 30:5

To my best friend and neighbor,
Cindy Sledge, my own "Pig Pal."
And to all the mothers who love their children,
even when they can't be with them.
You are not forgotten.

Chapter One

A hot, humid September wind whipped across the flat countryside as mourners dressed in fashionable funeral black filed out of the small country church just outside Plano, Texas. Mingling together beside the expensive sports cars and chauffeur-driven limousines lining the graveled driveway, the elite crowd talked in hushed, respectful tones.

Tricia Maria Dunaway looked around at the cream of Dallas society, here to say their final farewells to her father, the famous bull rider, Brant Dunaway. Her mind was numb with grief and shock; her eyes hidden behind dark sunglasses that did little to relieve the harsh glare of the bright Texas sun. Beside her, her fiancé Radford Randolph III, looking as dapper as always in his dark navy summer suit, stood with one arm solicitously touching her elbow.

"C'mon, honey," her grandfather, Harlan Dunaway, said, his usually firm voice shaky. "We've got to get back to the Hideaway. People'll be coming around to pay their respects and it's up to us to be there to greet them.''

Her mother, Pamela, pale and dark-haired, elegant and slender, in a black linen sheath and cultured pearls, nodded her agreement. ''Granddaddy's right, Trixie. We wouldn't want to be rude to all these good people who came to your daddy's funeral.''

Trixie looked straight ahead. ''No, Mama, Dunaways can't ever be rude, can we? I mean, what would people think?''

Pamela's brown eyes held a glint as cold and hard-edged as the huge marquis diamond in her necklace. ''I'm going to ignore that remark, Tricia Maria, only because I know losing your father has been a great strain on you.''

With a halfhearted effort, Trixie reached up a black-gloved hand to touch her mother's still smooth cheekbone. ''I'm sorry, Mama. I know you gave up a trip to Palm Beach to make it to Daddy's funeral. I guess I shouldn't be mean to you.''

''No, you shouldn't,'' Pamela retorted, her smile, exacted for the benefit of prying eyes, as intact as her unruffled classic bob. ''Even though your father and I were divorced, I still had feelings for the man.''

Trixie didn't respond. She'd heard it all too many times before. Too many times. Not even Rad's gentle endearments could bring her out of her deep grief.

She'd sat here in the church were she'd attended services all of her life and listened as Reverend Henry told them to rejoice in Brant's departure from this life.

''Be joyful,'' the good reverend told them. '''They that sow in tears shall reap in joy.'''

In spite of her faith, in spite of the strong Christian

values she'd been taught, Trixie couldn't feel any joy today. After all those many years of riding bucking, angry bulls and fighting his way into and out of barroom brawls, Brant Dunaway had lost his life to the one thing even he couldn't fight off or sweet-talk his way out of—heart disease.

How could she find any joy in that cold, simple fact? How could she find any joy at all, when in her heart she kept thinking she should have stayed close to her father. She should have made him go to the doctor, take care of himself, live to be an old man. But...instead, she'd stayed away from the ranch in Arkansas where he'd spent his last years isolated and alone. Now she felt the remorse and regret that came with his death. So final, so harsh. So cold. Without even a goodbye between them.

And this was just the beginning. Tomorrow she had to take her father's body back to Arkansas, back to the ranch he'd loved more than he'd ever loved the fancy mansion near Plano that everyone called Dunaway's Hideaway. The mansion, Victorian in style and stark white and lacy in design, had been more like an overdecorated birthday cake to her father. His real hideaway had always been the crude, run-down ranch in Arkansas he'd inherited from his mother's side of the family.

The ranch where he'd requested to be buried.

The ranch Trixie had inherited from him.

The ranch where Logan Maxwell worked as foreman.

Logan. His name still brought little tremors of awakening shooting through Trixie's system. Would he be waiting there to greet her when she brought

Brant home for the last time? Would he speak to her, acknowledge her, talk to her about the last eight years of his life?

Or…would Logan turn away from her in disgust, the way her father had turned away?

Harlan took her by the arm, gently urging her into the waiting, black limousine. "Let's get going, Trixie. It's a long ride back to the house."

Trixie nodded absently, then allowed Rad to guide her into the roomy car, her thoughts on the man she'd have to face once again, come tomorrow. "Yes, Granddaddy, it is a long way back. A very long way." Then she closed her eyes and thought about Logan…and remembered.

"But where's Daddy?" Trixie had asked Pamela as they dressed for her coming-out ball that spring night so long ago. "He's supposed to be here with you, to present me."

"Brant won't be attending the ball, sugar," Pamela retorted, her chin lifting a notch, her eyes capturing Trixie's in the gilt mirror of the dresser where she sat. Trixie stood in the center of the elaborate bedroom her mother shared with her father, that is, when they weren't fighting. Pamela then turned away, patting her upswept curls, to stare down into the velvet-lined jewel case set out on the Louis XIV dresser.

Disappointed and steaming mad, Trixie stormed toward her mother, her white taffeta skirts swishing over the Aubusson carpet, her blond curls contrasting sharply with her mother's darker ones. "Daddy wouldn't do that to me! He promised he'd be here."

Pamela pursed her lips as she gazed into the jewel

case. Making her selection, she lifted out a brilliant diamond necklace, then smiled over at Trixie. "Here, sweetie, wear this."

Trixie pushed the gaudy necklace away. "I'd prefer pearls, Mother, and I'd prefer you tell me what's going on here. Where's Daddy?"

Frustrated, Pamela snapped the jewel case shut. "And I'd really prefer not to discuss your father. Especially not now, right before your coming-out ball." Spinning on the satin-covered vanity stool, she stared up at her daughter with beseeching eyes. "Oh, Trixie, we've waited for this night all of your life, darling. Tonight you'll become a part of the best of Dallas society. Let's not spoil things by talking about your missing father."

Trixie stood there, her gaze sharp on her beautiful, haughty mother. "You had another fight with him, didn't you?"

"I said I don't want to talk about Brant."

"That's it! You picked a fight with him so he wouldn't want to come to my cotillion. How could you do that, Mother?"

Pamela's expression quickly changed from sweet to steely. "It wasn't just me, young lady. You know how your father can be. And this time he pushed me too far." Waving a diamond-clad hand, she added, "If Brant isn't here tonight, it's his own fault. Your grandfather will present you. And that's all I have to say on the matter."

The matter turned out to be divorce. Of course, Pamela didn't reveal that to Trixie until after the season was over, until after she'd been to so many debutante parties, and danced with so many fumble-footed sons of oil tycoons and banking CEOs, that she thought she'd literally scream. No, Trixie found out the horrible, awful truth on the day of her graduation from high school, when Pamela lifted her wine glass in a toast at the formal dinner party she'd arranged for "just family," then presented Trixie with a trip to Europe as a graduation gift.

"We leave in a week, darling. Just you and me. I'll show you all the best places, of course, and introduce you to my friends over there. We'll stay at a lovely chateau in France, and I've arranged for a private manor house in the English countryside. After we've done London, of course. You'll love Europe. I plan on introducing you to several very eligible bachelors."

Shocked, Trixie glanced around the long dining room of the Dunaway mansion, hoping to find some answers from either her beaming mother or her strangely quiet grandfather. "And what about Daddy?"

She didn't miss the meaningful gaze that moved between her mother and Harlan. In fact, she hadn't missed much over the past few weeks, in spite of being busy. Now she was sure something was going on. Brant hadn't even stayed for dinner. Her father, usually so carefree and talkative, usually so full of silly banter, seemed so distant, so quiet these days.

Earlier, he'd given her two beautiful graduation gifts, a golden heart necklace and one of his most prized possessions, his belt buckle from his last days as bull riding champ, and then he'd told her, "You know how much I love you, baby. But I've got to get on the road again. I just want you to know, Trixiebelle, how proud I am of you.'' She hadn't missed the catch in his voice or the sad look in his brilliant blue eyes.

Needing to know what was happening, and tired of being protected like a fragile child, she repeated her question. ''I said, what about Daddy? I've hardly seen him in the past four months, and today he rushed in for my graduation, but couldn't even stay for dinner tonight. Why does he keep coming home, only to leave again on business? He hasn't traveled this much since his prime rodeo days. Will he at least join us in Europe, Mama?''

''Your father hates Europe,'' Pamela explained. ''And besides, he wouldn't come if I begged him. In fact, now that you're through with graduation, you might as well know—your father has been spending a lot of his time up in Arkansas.''

''Arkansas?'' Trixie wasn't surprised to hear that, but she wondered what the big secret was. After all, Brant owned a huge chunk of land near Little Rock. ''Is he finally fixing up the ranch? Is that it?''

Another stern glance from Harlan, but it didn't stop her mother. Pamela shrugged, then tightened her expression into a firm frown. ''Well, he is wasting a fair amount of time and money on that broken-down hovel in the wilderness if that's what you mean. Trixie, your father has decided he wants to live up there permanently, and well…I can't agree to that. So I've put my foot down, and…we've decided it would be best if we go our separate ways and get a divorce—''

Trixie looked from her mother to Harlan. Her grandfather seemed to age right there in front of her. ''I'm sorry, honey. I didn't want you to find out this way," he said, his eyes watering up, his accusing gaze shifting to Pamela.

Shrugging daintily, Pamela rushed on. "I've fought against it and tried to keep up appearances, of course, but this marriage can't be fixed. No amount of prayer or reasoning is going to change Brant Dunaway into a decent, reasonable human being. I've discussed this thoroughly with Harlan, and he's been very generous about letting me continue to live here, for your sake. I've had counseling with Reverend Henry, but it's just too late. Your father expected me to give up my life here, everything I've come to love, everything I've worked so hard to achieve for both you and for this family, to go up there and live in the boonies." She waved a hand. "I'm too old and too established here to start over."

"I can't believe this," Trixie said, turning to her grandfather for support. "Do you agree with her?"

Harlan cleared his throat and sat back heavily in his Queen Anne chair. "I'm trying to remain neutral. I know how much that land means to your pappy, so I can't keep him from doing something he's wanted for such a long time. Heck, he's got more money than he'll ever need, what with my holdings and his own money from endorsements, but he's determined to do this thing his own way. He's basically told me to stay out of it." He glanced down the table at Pamela again. "But he sure wanted your mama to come up there with him. Thought it might do them good to get away from everything…and start over."

Trixie stared at her mother's unyielding face. "Couldn't you just try it, for a little while, Mama? It sounds like Daddy really wants to make things up to you."

"Hah!" Pamela interjected, her brown eyes flashing fire. "He should have thought about that years ago when he left me for weeks at a time to travel the rodeo circuit. You're right, Harlan. He never needed the money. We could have had a good life together, if he'd only given it a chance."

"And what about you, Mother?" Trixie said in a low, trembling voice. "Did you ever give him a chance? You know how much he loved being a bull rider, yet you never once supported him or gave him any encouragement. Why did you marry my daddy, anyway?"

Pamela looked her daughter straight in the eye. "I've often asked myself that same question. But I can tell you this, young lady, because I'm a Christian, I tried to make this marriage work. I guess some prayers just can't be answered."

Hurt and disgusted, Trixie turned back to Harlan. "How can you sit there and let her talk about your only son that way?"

Harlan lifted up out of his chair. "Your mother knows exactly how I feel about the subject of my son. I love Brant with all of my heart, and I'll continue to support his efforts up in Arkansas. But for your sake, and for the sake of this family, I can't very well put Pamela out on the street. We will continue to be discreet about this, and we will continue to act like Dunaways, regardless of any rift in this family."

Trixie shot up out of her chair, rattling dishes and upsetting water glasses in a very unladylike fashion that made her oh-so-proper mother wince. "I get it.

Close ranks and put our best face forward, no matter how torn apart this family really is. Show the world the perfect life of the Dunaways, the family everyone in Dallas can model their own miserable lives after, right? Pretend we're good, upstanding Christians who attend church every Sunday and give a hefty tithe each and every month.''

"That's enough, Tricia," Pamela said. "We are good people and we have nothing, nothing at all, to be ashamed of."

"Except the truth," Trixie retorted. "We're living a facade, a lie, Mother. And I for one, won't continue it." Slamming her linen dinner napkin down, she headed for the foyer, then turned to face her stunned mother and disapproving grandfather. "And I won't be going to Europe with you. I'm going to Arkansas, to see my father, and I intend to stay there until this fall. But don't worry, I'll be home in time for college. So you just keep on bragging to all of your friends. And while I'm gone, you can continue to keep up appearances to save face, Mother, since that seems to be so much more important to you than trying to save your marriage."

In the end, however, even Pamela's manipulations and sugar-coated half truths couldn't save face. When the Dallas press got wind of the impending divorce, things turned nasty, and Pamela turned vindictive. After demanding a multimillion-dollar settlement from Brant, Pamela went to Europe alone and made headlines by being seen with some very eligible men. Of course, Pamela managed to keep things highly proper and above reproach, stating that she loved her daughter and only wanted to protect Tricia Maria from all of this hurt and pain.

She never stopped to think how much she'd hurt both Trixie and her father. No, Pamela always managed to put a spin on the truth, to twist it to her advantage and to come out, as Harlan put it, "smelling like a rose."

So that summer Trixie went to Arkansas to find her own peace of mind, to regroup and reassess her life, to get back at her domineering, self-righteous mother, and to get reacquainted with the father she loved and adored.

And…wound up meeting a man who changed her life.

That summer Tricia Maria Dunaway fell in love with Logan Maxwell.

That fall Tricia Maria Dunaway did not enroll in college at Southern Methodist University, because she was expecting Logan Maxwell's child.

As the sleek limousine pulled into the long drive leading up to the mansion, Trixie glanced up to the sign over the white fretwork gate, proclaiming the surrounding thousand acres of prime Texas real estate to be Dunaway's Hideaway.

But Trixie knew in her heart, this was no hideaway. She knew she'd never be able to hide from the truth, no matter how secluded and protected her grandfather's estate might be, no matter how much power the Dunaway name carried in Texas, no matter how hard her mother had managed to put a pretty face on the worst of situations by guarding Trixie's great sin with all the alert attention and precise organization of a qualified damage control expert.

Even though no one, absolutely no one in Dallas, knew about the baby, especially not Rad's blue-blooded family, Trixie knew in her heart, knew in her soul, that somewhere out there she had a child. Once, she'd accused her mother of living a lie; now _she_ had to live one each and every day of her life. Unlike Pamela and Harlan, and even her father, she couldn't forever stay in a state of determined denial. It was her great secret, her great burden to bear. She had yet to forgive herself for her one youthful indiscretion, or for allowing those around her to force her to let her child be sent away like a parcel of dirty laundry. Sometimes, she lay awake at night, asking God to show her the way, to give her comfort, to help her bear the sorrow of her secret. And she wondered, did God ever hear her pleas? Or like her misguided mother, was she praying for all the wrong things?

But tomorrow, tomorrow when she at last faced Logan again, as much as she now believed in the absolute truth, she hoped the truth wouldn't be plastered there on her own face. Because he could never know the truth.

Logan could never, ever know that she'd been forced to give his child up for adoption. Only she and her immediate family could ever know that great shame. Because of the Dunaway power, Logan hadn't had a say in the matter, at all. He had no idea that a baby had even been conceived.

Again, Reverend Henry's words came back to haunt her.

"They that sow in tears shall reap in joy."

Dear God, she silently prayed now, hidden behind her dark glasses, shielded by the touch of Rad's hand on her own, *Will I ever be forgiven? How can I face Logan, knowing what I did? How can I enter into marriage with Rad, with a such a devastating secret between us? How can I ever be whole again?*

Tomorrow she would take Brant Dunaway's remains back to the place he loved most. Tomorrow, she would come face-to-face with her past and the man she had once loved so fiercely.

As Rad helped Trixie out of the car, the unmerciful Texas wind whipped her hair and sang mournfully in her ear, holding her, pulling her close. But Trixie fought at the wind, her thoughts turning to the rolling green hills of Arkansas. And she desperately wished she could turn back time.

Chapter Two

Time might have changed Trixie, but time had not changed the ranch. The red-stained, open barn still stood at a slanted angle beside the dirt lane, looking as if the next strong wind might just knock it over. But Trixie knew this old barn had weathered everything, from gentle rains to fierce, whirling tornadoes. And yet it stood.

Off to the right were the big rectangular stables, their planked walls painted the same aged red shade as the barn. As the wind rushed through the long, cool stable corridors, the smell of fresh hay and pungent manure assaulted her senses and touched her with such a sensory remembrance, she had to close her eyes to keep the tears from falling. She could almost hear her father's deep-throated laughter floating along on that wind. She could see herself and Logan, young and carefree, walking the horses, cleaning the stalls, stealing a kiss in a dark, cool alcove.

Out beyond the barn and stables, out beyond the

screened-in cookhouse and the narrow barracks that served as the bunkhouse, the pine-covered hills that formed the beginnings of the Ouachita Mountains lifted and flowed like a green velvet blanket tossed across a rumpled bed.

Everything about the place that Brant had simply called The Ranch, was rumpled and slightly off center. It was as run-down and down home as they came. Nothing fancy, no frills—just a good, solid working ranch that included cattle, sheep and pigs, along with corn, cotton, produce and hay. Certainly nothing to be ashamed of, but nothing to shout about, either, as her father used to say.

Pamela had always hated this place.

Trixie had always loved it.

And missed it.

Now she stepped out of the rental car she'd picked up at the Little Rock airport, to look toward the west where the small lodge stood on a pine-shaded hillside. Brant had built his modest house there, so he could wake up each morning with a perfect view of the surrounding peaks and valleys. Off in the distance the mountains presented a muted, watercolor vista of rock and trees. Brant had loved his view of this part of the Ozark Plateau. He had liked seeing his little domain as he stood on the wide, posted porch with his first cup of coffee.

Now, the A-frame, log-cabin-style house looked forlorn and lonesome, a bittersweet reminder to Trixie of all that she had lost. Her father had built the house as a retreat for Pamela, hoping to mend the great tear in their doomed marriage. But Pamela had shunned his gift and him. Trixie wondered if her mother felt any guilt or remorse over that now. She knew she certainly did.

In a few hours the meager staff would gather together not far from the brown-logged lodge, underneath a great live oak that stood alone like a sentinel on one of those rolling hills, to watch Branton Nelson Dunaway be put to rest in the earth he loved. Trixie had arrived early to make sure everything had been arranged. The funeral home in Little Rock would bring her father's remains in a few hours.

Right now she needed this time to readjust to being here, to steel herself against seeing Logan again. She just wanted to stand here in the sandy driveway and look out over what now belonged to her.

Rad wanted her to sell it, take the money and run.

"We won't have time to fool with some run-down ranch in Arkansas, darling. We'll be so busy with my law practice and your consulting work I don't see how you can be in two places at once."

"I won't have to be there, Rad. The Ranch has a very capable foreman."

"That Maxwell fellow? You don't even know him that well. For all we know he might decide to take you for a ride now that Brant's gone. From everything Harlan's told me, the place barely breaks even as it is. No, I think it'd be best to get rid of it. We'll invest the money. I'll call my broker first thing once you've taken care of the sale."

Trixie closed her eyes and leaned back against the rented Nissan, images of the past she'd tried to bury springing up like wildflowers in her mind. Was that why she'd considered selling the ranch—to get rid of any traces of her great shame? Now she had to wonder why she'd even agreed to sell it at all. How in the world could she tell Logan that she wanted to sell the land he loved so much, the only home he'd known since he was a teenager?

Logan Maxwell heard the slam of a car door on the other side of the barn. Dropping his paintbrush, he found a rag on a nearby shelf and tried unsuccessfully to clean the white paint off his hands. Then he headed toward the front of the building, his heart pumping, his nerve endings on full alert, his whole body coiled tightly against seeing the woman he knew would be waiting on the other side.

Trixie.

Then he saw her standing there with her eyes closed and her head thrown back as she invited the wind to kiss her face. She wore designer jeans and a pair of hand-tooled buttery tan boots—he would bet she'd had them specially made in Austin, and a bright pink-and-green-colored Western-style shirt—probably a Panhandle Slim—and she looked about as out of place as a Barbie doll at a G.I. Joe convention.

She also looked beautiful. Her hair was still that same honeyed hue of blond, although she'd cut it— no, she'd paid an overpriced hairdresser to cut it—to a becoming, layered bob that framed her face with sleek flips and soft swirls. Still tall and cool, still the darling of Dallas, still the belle of the ball. He couldn't see her eyes, but he knew the color was a deep, pure blue, same as the Arkansas sky over his head. He couldn't take his own eyes away from her, though, so he leaned there against the support of the rickety barn and allowed himself this one concession while he compared the real-life woman to the girl he'd watched walk away so long ago.

He'd had an image of this woman in his mind for the past eight years, an image that had warred within his subconscious, an image that at times had haunted him, at other times had comforted him. He'd tried so very hard to put Tricia Maria out of his mind. But she wouldn't disappear. It had taken her father's death to bring her back to him in the flesh.

Now he used bitterness as his only weapon against the surge of emotions threatening to erupt throughout his system.

He had so many questions; he needed so many answers.

So he remained silent and just stared at her.

Trixie opened her eyes, feeling the heat from the sun on her tear-streaked face at about the same time she felt someone watching her. It didn't take her long to figure out who that someone was.

Logan.

She stared across the expanse of the dirt driveway, to the spot where he leaned with his arms crossed over his chest, just inside the open barn doors. In her mind she held the memory of a young man in his early twenties, muscled and tanned, with thick wisps of brown hair falling across his impish, little-boy face. This Logan was the same as the one in her memories, yet different. He still wore his standard uniform of faded Levi's and chewed up Ropers she remembered in her dreams. A battered Stetson, once tan, now a mellow brown, sat on his head. The torn T-shirt, smeared with grease and dirt, told her he still worked as hard as anybody around there, and…he obviously still wore the attitude, the whole-world's-out-to-do-me-in attitude, that had attracted her to him in the first place.

Only now, a new layer had been added to his essence, along with the crow's feet and the glint in his brown-black eyes. He'd matured into a full-grown man, his muscles heavier, more controlled, broader, his expression hardened, more intense, deeper.

He looked bitter and angry and hurt.

He looked delicious and vulnerable and lost.

And he looked as if he'd rather be any place on earth except standing there with her.

"Hello, Logan," she said, her voice sounding lost and unsure to her own ears as it drifted up through the live oaks.

"Tricia Maria." He lifted away from the barn to stalk toward her, his eyes never leaving her face. When he'd gotten to within two feet of her, he stopped and hooked his thumbs in the stretched, frayed belt loops of his jeans. "Sorry about your daddy."

"Yeah, me, too." She looked away, out over the hills. "He wanted to be buried here, so…"

"So you had no choice but to come back."

"Yes, I had to—for him, for his sake."

Not for me. Not for my sake, Logan thought. Because she'd written him off a long time ago. And they both knew why. Yet he longed to ask her.

The questions buzzed around them like hungry bees. Logan wanted to lash out at her, to ask her why, why she'd left him so long ago. But he didn't. Because he knew the answer, knew probably even better than she did why she'd deserted him and left him, and lied to him. Instead he said, ''C'mon. We'll get your stuff up to the lodge. When's this thing taking place?''

''Three o'clock,'' she said, understanding he meant the graveside service for her father. ''Didn't anybody call you about it?''

He didn't look at her as he moved around her to get into the driver's side of the car. ''Yeah, some fellow named Ralph, Raymond—''

''Rad. Radford Randolph. He's…we're engaged. I asked him to call ahead and let you know when we'd get here. Granddaddy's coming later.''

Logan slid into the car, then patted the passenger's seat, his dark gaze on her face. ''Get in. I'll drive you up to the lodge.''

Trixie had no choice but to do as he asked. She remembered that about Logan. Quiet, alert, a man of few words. Dark and brooding. A rebel. A trouble-maker who'd been turned over to her father for a job over ten years before by a judge who'd agreed with Brant, and Logan's mother, Gayle, not to send him to a juvenile home. He'd come to work off a truancy sentence, and he'd never left.

In spite of everything, Logan had not deserted her father the way she had, the way Pamela had. Some-how, that had comforted her and made her resent him at the same time. Logan had known Brant Dunaway better than Brant's own flesh and blood. She could tell he was taking this hard, too. Maybe that was why he had a scowl on his scarred, harsh face. Out of respect, Trixie didn't speak again. Besides, she didn't know what to say, how to comfort him. She'd prayed long and hard to find some sort of comfort for herself, but it hadn't come yet.

Logan pulled the car up to the long, square lodge that Brant had built with his own hands, then turned in the seat to stare over at Trixie. "Yeah, this Rad fellow was more than happy to talk with me a spell. Asked a lot of questions, too."

Frowning, Trixie said, "What kind of questions?"

Logan tipped his battered hat back on his head and wrapped one hair-dusted arm across the steering wheel, his eyes full of accusation. "Oh, about profit and loss, how much income we've been generating, how much I think the land is worth."

Trixie moaned and closed her eyes. How could Rad be so presumptuous? This wasn't his land, after all. It was hers.

When she felt Logan's hand on her chin, she opened her eyes to find him close, too close. His touch, so long remembered, so long denied, brought a great tearing pain throughout her system. To protect her frayed nerve endings, and the small amount of pride she had left, she tried to pull away.

He forced her head around so she had to look at him. "You're gonna sell out, aren't you?"

She did manage to push his hand away then, but the current of awareness remained as an imprint on her skin. "I...I haven't decided."

Logan jerked open the door and hauled his big body out of the car, then turned to bend down and glare at her again. "I can't believe you'd even think of selling this place, but then again, maybe I should have seen it coming."

"What's that supposed to mean?" she asked, her

hand flying to the door handle. When he didn't answer her, she rounded the car to meet him at the trunk. "Logan, explain that last remark, please?"

Logan opened the trunk, then snorted at the many travel bags she'd brought along. "Still so cool, calm and collected, still the fashionable big-city girl, aren't you, Trixie?"

In defense of herself she said, "I wasn't sure how long I'd need to stay."

He lifted her suitcases out of the trunk, then slammed the lid shut. "Oh, I think I can clarify that for you, darlin'. Just long enough to shed yourself of this place, I imagine." When she looked away, he grabbed her arm to spin her around. "Am I right, Trixie? Is that it? Were you planning on pulling another vanishing act, like you did all those years ago?"

"No," she said, humiliation and rage causing her to grit her teeth. "No."

He pressed her close to the car's back. "Yes. I say yes. As soon as you can sell this place to the highest bidder, you'll tuck tail and head back to Dallas." Hefting her suitcases up with a grunt, he added, "After all, some things never change, do they, sweetheart?"

She was surprised to find that some changes had been made to the ranch, after all, such as the tiny white chapel Brant had built by the great oak where he wanted to be buried, and she was even more surprised by the large turnout for her father's graveside service. Trixie knew her father had a lot of friends back in Dallas, but here? She'd always imagined him alone and reclusive, once he'd lost touch with his

family, but then again Brant Dunaway hadn't been
the kind of man to be satisfied with his own company
for too long. Brant had loved life; had loved moving
and roaming and watching and experiencing. What
was it Granddaddy used to say? He was a good ol'
boy with a big ol' heart.

Only, Pamela had never seen that. She only saw
what she termed Brant's weaknesses; his flaws and
failings far outweighed his goodness in Pamela's
eyes. Once the novelty of being married to the renegade rodeo hero son of an oil man had worn off, she'd
judged him with a very harsh measure; he'd never
stood a chance of living up to Pamela's standards.

Trixie had always been confused by her mother's
double standards. Pamela professed to being a Christian, attended church each Sunday, did all the right
things, yet she never seemed to possess the one basic
trait that made anyone a true Christian. Pamela had
never learned tolerance or acceptance. She'd tried to
change Brant, and it had backfired on her. And she
was now working hard on her daughter.

Right up till this morning, when, in a nervous tizzy
she'd tried her level best to talk Trixie out of coming.
"Trixie, I just don't think it's wise for you to go back
to that place. Harlan can take care of the burial. Stay
here with me, sugar, and help me plan your engagement party."

"I'm going, Mother, and that's final. I want to be
there to see Daddy buried. And I have to decide about
what to do."

"Get rid of that land as fast as you can. You and
Rad don't need the bother, darling. You're going to

be busy, too busy to have to deal with that old headache of a ranch.''

Pamela would never come out and say it, but she
didn't want her daughter anywhere near Logan Maxwell again. Pamela had erased the whole episode from
her mind like a bad movie.

Now, as Trixie watched the long line of people
marching across the hillside toward the spot where
Brant would be buried, she was glad her mother
would not be among the crowd. She needed this time
alone with her father, one last time. Her granddaddy
was here, though, right by her side as he'd always
been, his old eyes watering up as he looked at the
shiny new walnut-grained casket, encased with a set
of brass bull horns, where his son now rested.

''Are you all right?'' Trixie asked Harlan, worried
about him. Her grandfather had started out as a wild-
catter and had gone on to build an oil empire. He'd
paid his dues; done his time. He was getting old. And
his only son's death had aged him both physically and
emotionally.

''I'm fine, honey. Just missing your father.''

''Me, too.'' She looked down at the sunflower
wreath lying across the closed casket. ''I should have
visited him more—stayed in touch. I should have let
him know I cared.''

''He knew you loved him.''

''Did he? Did he really know that?'' she asked.

''Yes, he surely did. I kept in touch with him, you
know. After all, he was my son. And, thank the Lord,
we made our peace with each other long before he
died.''

''Did...did he ever talk about me?''

Harlan lifted his gaze to her face, his blue eyes, so like his son's, full of love and compassion. "All the time, honey. All the time."

Trixie saw the hesitation in her grandfather's expression. He seemed to want to say more, but instead he just looked away, down at the ground. At least he'd told her that her father still thought about her and acknowledged her existence. Trixie found some comfort in that.

After she'd had the baby—they'd never allowed her to know whether it had been a boy or a girl— Brant had drifted further and further out of her life. Still numb, still grieving over the twist her life had taken, she went on to college, a year late. Determined to get her life back on track, she'd soon became immersed in her studies and her somewhat vague social life. She'd gone through all the motions—the sororities, the campus parties, the whirl of college life, but her heart, her center always came back here to her father...and to Logan. Ashamed, she'd felt as though neither wanted anything to do with her, so she hadn't made any effort to mend the shattered relationships with the two men she loved and respected most in all the world.

Logan stood now, apart from all the others, with a group of about eight children of various ages. Watching him, Trixie wondered again how this was affecting him. Brant had been like a father to him. Logan's mother, Gayle, had come to the ranch years ago, divorced and struggling with a rebellious teenage son. Brant had given her a job as cook and housekeeper, and promptly had put her son to work on the ranch.

The arrangement had worked, since Brant hadn't

spent too much time at the ranch back then. He'd
depended on Gayle and Logan to watch over things,
along with some locals he hired to tend the animals
and crops. By the time Trixie arrived that summer so
long ago, however, Brant was a permanent resident
here, and he and Logan had formed a grudging respect for each other. That mutual respect had seen
them through the worst of times. The very worst of
times.

Not wanting to delve too deeply into those particular memories, Trixie turned her attention to the hap-
hazard group of children around Logan. "Granddaddy, who are all those youngsters?"

Harlan cleared his throat and glanced in the direction of the silent, solemn group. "They're living on
the ranch, Tricia Maria. They've been here for most
of the summer."

Shocked, Trixie stared hard at her grandfather.
"Why? I mean, are they helping out with the crops
as a project? Did Logan give them jobs?"

Harlan started to speak again when the preacher
lifted his hands to gather the group around Brant's
casket. Harlan leaned close and whispered, "I'll explain it all later."

There was no easy explanation for death, especially
when speaking to a child. Logan stood with the children he was in charge of and wondered again if he'd
handled any of this in the right way. Granted, he'd
had training in counseling youths from the minister
who was about to conduct Brant's funeral service. But
talking with children was never easy. Children demanded complete and total honesty, and sometimes

adults, by trying to protect them, hedged and pawed around the truth. Logan certainly knew all about that.

Looking over at Trixie now, Logan felt a stab of guilt. He hadn't exactly been completely truthful with her, but then again, she had kept her distance, and her secret, from him all these years, too. As he watched her now, so cool and pulled together in her black linen pantsuit, he had to wonder what her intentions were. How could she come barreling in here again after all these years and rearrange his whole way of life?

Feeling a tug on the sleeve of his chambray shirt, Logan looked down to find ten-year-old Marco holding on to him.

"Hey, buddy," Logan said on a low whisper. "How ya doing?"

Marco, a beautiful Hispanic child whose mother had abandoned him when he was three, shook his shiny black-haired head and said, "Not too good, Mr. Logan." He put a hand to his heart. "It hurts here, inside. I miss Mr. Brant."

"Yeah, me, too, bud," Logan replied, his voice tight, his words clipped. "Tell you what, though. You just stand here by me and hold tight to my hand, okay? We'll get through this together. Then later I'll bring out Radar and let you exercise him around the paddock. Deal?"

Marco's sad expression changed into a grin. "I get to ride the pony?"

Logan gave the boy a conspiring wink. "You and you alone, partner."

Marco took his hand and held on. Soon, all of the children had shifted closer to Logan. Their warmth soothed the great hole in his soul and made him even more determined to hold on to what he'd helped Brant build here. Then he saw Caleb standing by Gayle. Motioning for the seven-year-old boy, Logan waited as the youngest of the group ran and sailed into his arms, then wrapped his arms around Logan's neck. Holding the boy close, Logan decided right then and there that he had to talk some sense into Tricia Maria Dunaway. He wouldn't stand by and let her sell this ranch. Not after everything that had passed between them. With that thought in mind, he glanced over at Trixie and held tight to the little brown-haired boy in his arms.

She chose that moment to look up, her eyes meeting his in a silent battle of longing and questions. Soon he'd have his answers, Logan decided. And maybe soon she'd have hers, too. Whether she liked it or not.…

Then the minister preached to them about finding their answers through the word of God. ''For the Lord is good, his mercy is everlasting, and his truth endureth to all generations.''

The truth. Could it endure between Trixie and him? Was it time to find out? Logan stared across at the woman he'd tried so hard to forget and wondered if someone up there was trying to send him a personal message.

Much later, after all the mourners had paid their respects, after Harlan had headed back down the hill to the lodge to rest a spell, after the sun had dipped behind the distant live oaks and loblolly pines, Trixie stood alone beside her father's freshly dug grave and remembered all the good and wonderful things about Brant Dunaway.

And she cried. She'd never felt so lost and alone.

Until she felt a hand on her arm.

Turning, she saw Logan standing there, his eyes as dark and rich as the land beneath their feet, his expression a mixture of sympathy and bitterness. He didn't speak; didn't offer her any pretty platitudes or pat condolences. Instead, he simply stood there beside her and let her cry.

And finally, when she could stand it no longer, when he could hold back no longer, he took her in his arms and held her while the red-gold September sun slipped reluctantly behind the Arkansas hills.

Chapter Three

"He used to bring me daisies on my birthday," Trixie said later as they sat on a nearby hillside.

The shadows of dusk stretched out before them, darkness playing against the last, shimmering rays of the sun. Off in the distance, a cow lowed softly, calling her calf home for supper. Trixie stared across the widening valley, her gaze taking in the panoramic view of the beautiful burgundy-and-white Brangus cattle strolling along, dipping their great heads to graze the grasslands.

"He always did like wildflowers," Logan answered. "Remind me to show you the field of sunflowers he planted just over the ridge. The wreath on his casket came from those."

Trixie glanced over at the man sitting beside her. Logan had brought her such a comfort, coming back up here to sit with her. "Thank you," she said at last.

"For what?"

"For not pushing me. For just being you."

He snorted, then threw down the blade of grass he'd been chewing on. Glancing toward her, he said, "I thought me just being me was the reason you never came back here."

Not ready to discuss that particular issue, she ran a hand through her hair and leaned her chin down on her bent knees. "I had a lot of reasons for not coming back here, Logan."

He'd like to know each and every one of them. But he didn't press her. That wasn't his style. "Yeah, well, we all have our reasons for doing the things we do, sugar." He looked away, out over the lush farmland. "I take full responsibility for what happened back then, Trixie."

Shocked, she glanced over at him. Did he know about the baby, after all? "What do you mean?"

Logan looked back at her then, his dark eyes shining with regret and longing. "Our one time together—I should have stopped before things got so out of control."

"I played a part in that night, too, Logan." And paid dearly for it. She shrugged, hoping to push the hurtful memories away. "Besides, it's over now."

"Is it?"

She looked down at her clenched hands, not wanting him to see the doubt and fear in her eyes. "It has to be. We were young and foolish back then and we made a mistake. We're adults now. We just have to accept the past and go on."

He nodded, then lowered his head. "Well, one thing is still clear—our lives are still very different. That much hasn't changed. Just like then. You were the boss's daughter, and I took advantage of that. I won't do it this time around.''

Ignoring his loud and clear message, she reminded him, ''No, you didn't do anything I didn't let you do.''

''Yeah, well, I could have been more careful.'' His voice grew deeper, the anger apparent in his next words. ''Then you saved my hide by begging your father not to fire me. The rich girl helping the poor, unfortunate stable hand.''

She realized where some of his bitterness was coming from. By asking Brant not to fire him after he'd caught them together, she'd only added insult to injury. ''You needed your job. Your mother would have been heartbroken if Daddy had sent you away.''

''So you went away instead.'' His eyes burned through her. ''I've had to live with that all of these years. I've had to live with a lot of things.''

Trixie reached out a hand to his arm, wanting to comfort him. What would he do, what would he think if he knew everything? ''Logan, I'm sorry.''

''Don't apologize! I'm the one who blew it!'' Suddenly afraid of being this near to her, of being this intimate with her, he hopped up to brush the dirt off the back of his jeans. ''C'mon. You must be hungry. Mama's probably got supper on the table by now.''

Trixie took the hand he offered down to her, her eyes meeting his in the growing dusk. With a firm tug, he had her up and standing in front of him. Too close. Logan dropped her hand, then turned without a word to stomp away.

She followed, wondering if she'd ever be able to figure out Logan Maxwell. She'd seen him at the service this afternoon, watching her with that bitter expression on his face. And…she'd seen him with the children. He obviously cared about his little wards. Especially that little boy who'd clung to him the entire time. What a cutie. Trixie had only glanced at the child briefly and then he'd been lost in the crowd of people trailing by to pay their respects.

"Tell me about the children," she said now as she hurried to catch up with him. "Grandfather said he'd explain. But I want you to."

Logan stopped to whirl around and stare at her. "You mean, you don't know?"

"Know what?"

"That this ranch is now a part-time foster home for troubled kids?"

"What?" Shocked, she looked around as if searching for some sort of justification. "Well, no. No one bothered to tell me anything about that." Sighing, she added, "I'm so tired of everyone trying to protect me. Why don't *you* tell me all about it."

Logan kept walking, but slowed his pace to a comfortable gait. "Your father wanted the ranch to be a place where people could come and learn about nature and about life. Through a program with the local church, he set up a foundation called The Brant Dunaway International Farm. We grow food and livestock for underprivileged countries, and we train volunteers to go into the villages of these countries and teach the locals how to live off the land. Most of what we produce here is shipped out of the country to help these people."

Trixie had to let that soak in. Her father, the rowdy

cowboy, doing missionary work for the church. "I don't believe it."

"I can't believe you weren't aware of it."

"The only thing I heard from the lawyers was that I had inherited this land. Everything else got lost in the fog shrouding my brain." Her head down, she added, "And well...I haven't exactly kept in touch over the years."

"Yeah, and who's fault is that?"

Frustrated and unable to tell him her reasons for staying away, she said, "Could we just get back to the children?"

He shot her a hard look. "Ah, the children. Does having them here bother you?"

She didn't miss the sarcasm in his question. "Well, no. I just want to know what's going on."

"These kids come to us through the church—from broken homes, from foster homes, from parents who've abandoned them, from law officers trying hard to save them. Most of them are juvenile offenders—petty stuff, like stealing from the local convenience store or vandalism. Small-time crimes that could lead to worse, if someone doesn't intervene. They've seen some ugly things out there beyond our front gates."

He stopped, taking a long breath. "We try to fix them—teach them pride and self-esteem, and how to be responsible and productive. We're like a summer camp, only," he glared over at her here, "only not for the rich and privileged few who can afford such luxuries. We cater to those who might never get a chance like this, and as corny as it might sound to someone like you, we try to teach them that there is some beauty and good in God's world.''

''As hard as it might be for someone like you to believe,'' she said, her words tight and controlled, ''I do have a social conscience, and I do care about the other human beings existing on this earth alongside me.''

''Really?''

''Yes, really. I just had no idea my father had such…such lofty ambitions toward saving the world.''

''He didn't try to save the world, Trixie. He just tried to make a difference on his own little piece of earth. And he worked long and hard and gave a lot of his own money to accomplish his goals. Things here were just starting to turn around when he got sick.''

''He worked himself to death, didn't he?''

Logan heard the anguish in her question, but couldn't find any sympathy for her pain. It was too little, too late now. ''Yeah, Brant worked hard, as hard as anybody on this place. It was like…it was like he was trying to work off all his demons, you know.''

''I do know,'' she said, understanding more than ever what her father must have gone through. It didn't help to know some of his pain had come from her own foolish actions. ''I wish—''

''Too late for wishes, sweetheart,'' Logan said as they reached the house. Then he stopped just before the screened back door, and turned to face her. ''But…it's not too late for you to continue with your father's dream. That is, if you don't sell this place right out from under us.''

''I haven't made a firm decision yet,'' she said on a defensive note.

He smiled then, showing her the dimples she remembered so well. ''That's all I needed to hear,'' he said on a low whisper.

His whisper, so soft, so sure, and his nearness, so exciting, so frightening, told Trixie that she was in for a long, hard battle. And she wasn't sure if she had the strength to fight both Logan *and* her guilt.

She only hoped God would show her the right way to deal with this.

Gayle Maxwell was a petite, dark-headed woman who, because of the hard life she'd had, looked older than her fifty-one years. Trixie watched Logan's mother, physically feeling the woman's disapproval of her presence there. Gayle had not been pleased all those years ago when Trixie and Logan had formed an instant bond; she apparently wasn't pleased now to have Trixie back in their lives. And, Trixie had to remind herself, the woman was probably concerned that soon she might be displaced and unemployed. Well, Trixie was worried about that, too.

''Hello, Mrs. Maxwell,'' Trixie said as they entered the long, paneled kitchen of the lodge. ''I'm sorry I didn't get a chance to speak with your earlier.''

''Hello, Tricia,'' Gayle replied, her lips tight, her red-rimmed eyes looking everywhere but at Trixie. ''Sorry about Brant. We'll all miss your daddy.''

''Me, too.''

Trixie knew Gayle had been avoiding her, but she

wasn't prepared for the woman's evasiveness tonight. Gayle looked downright uncomfortable. Her movements were erratic and jittery. Her brown eyes darted here and there, as if she expected someone to burst into the room and interrupt their meal any minute. Maybe Gayle was still upset about Brant's death. They had always had a close relationship.

Wanting to soothe the older woman, Trixie asked, "Can I do anything to help with dinner?"

Gayle turned back to the stove. "No, everything's under control." Over her shoulder she said to Logan, "I've already fed all of the children. Samantha's with them down at the bunkhouse, helping them with their studies."

Trixie watched as Logan nodded, then told her that Samantha was a trained counselor who helped out during the summer. "She's also a qualified teacher. Some of the kids aren't ready to go back into the mainstream just yet, so we homeschool them." He glanced at her, then back to his mother. "Where's… where's Caleb?"

Gayle dropped the spoon she'd been holding with a clatter. "Down at the bunkhouse with the rest," she said, her gaze holding her son's.

Trixie didn't miss the look that passed between mother and son, nor did she understand what was going on. She was tired and still stunned by her father's death and having to be here again, but it was obvious that these two had mixed feelings about her visit to the ranch. Not wanting to ask too many questions too soon, she could only lift her brows in a questioning expression.

By way of an explanation, Logan turned to Trixie.

"Caleb's the youngest of the bunch, so he spends a lot of time up here with Mama."

Trixie nodded. "Oh, the little boy you were holding at the funeral." With a poor attempt at humor, she added, "Goodness, he looks too adorable to be a juvenile offender. What's he in for?"

A dark look colored Logan's face. "His mother abandoned him," he said in a low, tight voice.

Trixie fell down on a chair, all the energy she had left quickly pooling at her feet. Logan's words felt like a slap against her suddenly hot skin. Of course, he had no way of knowing how close to home his words had hit. "How awful," she said, her words barely above a whisper. "He's so young, so little." *So like the child I gave up.*

Gayle turned then to stare over at her, the look on the older woman's face full of fear mixed with contempt. "Your Daddy told the boy he'd always have a home here. That is, unless you sell it out from under him."

"Mama, hush," Logan said, shooting Gayle a warning glare.

Trixie stood up then, determined to be firm and fair in dealing with the Maxwells. "I haven't made a decision regarding what to do about this place yet, Mrs. Maxwell. You see, I wasn't aware of the foundation my father had set up here."

"You would have been, if you'd bothered keeping in touch," Gayle said over her shoulder. "But I guess you had better things to do with your time."

Trixie's gaze flew to Logan's face. He looked uncomfortable, but it was obvious from his cold, restrained look that he agreed with his mother.

"You're absolutely right," she said, her heart breaking all over again to think that Logan felt this way about her. "I didn't stay close with my father, and I have only myself to blame for that, but now I'm trying to piece things together so I can make the right choice."

Gayle whirled then, her eyes full of distrust. "The right choice for all of us, or for yourself?" Before Trixie could answer, the woman barreled ahead. "I know all about your fancy degree, Ms. Dunaway. And I guess you're about as qualified and entitled as anybody to make changes at this place. Marketing consultant, is it? Fancy education, fancy title, fancy everything. But that don't make you smart. Not in my eyes, at least."

Shaking her spoon at Trixie, she added, "Your daddy used to say that it's better to be kind than wise and that true wisdom begins with kindness. Brant had both of those qualities down pat. Too bad his only daughter never learned them."

Tears pricked at Trixie's eyes, but she refused to let Gayle or Logan see her pain. After all, she couldn't just blurt out that she'd had a child out of wedlock with Logan and that her father had stopped talking to her afterward, and that was the reason she'd been forced to stay away from the ranch.

"Well, maybe I can learn all about kindness and wisdom while I'm here," she said in a quiet voice. "And I assure you, I won't make a hasty decision until I've weighed all of the facts."

Mustering what little dignity she had left, she carefully walked around the table, then edged her way to the open back door. "I'm not really very hungry, after all. If you'll both excuse me, I think I'd just like to go for a walk before I go to bed.''

Then she was out the door, out in the night air. The wind hit her skin, cooling the heat that radiated from her face, soothing the humiliation that radiated from her soul. From inside, she could hear Logan arguing with his mother, bits of scattered words echoing out over the trees. Was he arguing in her defense, or was he simply warning Gayle to tread lightly while the wicked witch was on the premises?

Trixie didn't bother sticking around to find out which. Instead she headed down the sandy dirt lane to the stables, her feet taking her where her mind wanted to be. From the single security light shining out over the trees and shrubbery, she found her way to the looming structure to seek shelter from all of her problems, just as she'd done that summer so long ago.

As Trixie entered the corridor of the long building, a slender mare, a working quarter horse, greeted her with a soft whinny and a toss of her white mane.

Reaching out to rub the nose of the chestnut-colored animal, Trixie cooed softly. ''Hello, girl. How ya doing?''

The animal nudged her hand in response.

Looking around for a feed bag, Trixie said, ''Let me see. I'll bet we can find you some sort of snack.''

For the next few minutes Trixie stood letting the mare eat the mixture of oats, bran and hay she'd found nearby. As she watched the animal munch, she remembered other times she'd done this same thing, always with Logan by her side. He knew everything there was to know about horses, and he'd learned it all from her father. Again she felt that stab of jealousy and resentment whenever she thought about Brant and Logan, here together like a father and son.

"Maybe I should have been born a boy," she said to herself, knowing in her heart that Brant had loved her once just the way she was. No, she couldn't hold a grudge for something she had forced her father to do. She had asked Brant to allow Logan to stay on, had begged him not to fire Logan.

"It's all my fault, Daddy," she had said at the time. "I…I flirted with him. I wanted to be with him. If you send him away, Gayle will go with him. Then they won't have a place to live. Please, Daddy, don't do this. I'll go…I'll go back to Dallas, and I promise I won't have anything to do with Logan again."

She'd always believed she'd done Logan a favor. Now she had to wonder if instead she'd done him a great disservice by fighting his fight for him. But in the end it didn't really matter. She'd made the best decision, based on her love for Logan at the time.

Now she had the power to destroy everything that was left between them. She wanted to be rid of her past. That was why she'd been determined to sell this place. And now she'd come face-to-face with that past again, but there was so much more to have to deal with, so much responsibility being thrown on her shoulders.

Her first instinct was to run as far away from this place as she could possibly get. If she got involved in Brant's dreams for this ranch, she'd be up to her eyeballs in something that might quite possibly become an overwhelming burden. Yet if she didn't at least think about keeping the ranch and continuing her father's work here, she'd never forgive herself.

Was she up to the task? Could she face down the secrets of her past with Logan, for the sake of her father's dream and for the sake of these children who'd been entrusted to his care?

Without warning, little Caleb's cherubic face came to mind. She couldn't get the picture of the little boy who'd been clinging to Logan out of her head. What would happen to Caleb if she sold the ranch?

How could she make such an important decision when she was so very tired and confused? The big mare snorted, her brown eyes giving away no secrets as she nuzzled Trixie's hand with her wet nose.

"Guess I need to pray hard," Trixie said to the animal. "That's what Granddaddy always tells me to do when I have a problem."

She let the mare finish the last of the mash, then dusted her wet hand against her pants before she walked on through the stables. When she came to the little tack room, Trixie stopped and closed her eyes against the intensity of her memories, the smell of saddle soap and horse sweat blending together in her mind. It was here in this very room, where Logan had first kissed her. She'd fallen in love that summer— her first love. But it wasn't meant to be. Now she had Rad and her life with him was all planned out. Everyone said they made a perfect couple.

Trixie closed her eyes. *Help me make the right decision, Lord.*

When she opened her eyes, Logan was standing in the doorway watching her, his own eyes devoid of any condemnation or judgment. For just a moment, it was as if time had stopped and they were back there, young and carefree and exploring the raging emotions coursing between them. But Trixie had to remind herself that that time was over.

Logan, however, had other considerations on his mind. He walked toward her with a purposeful look on his face, then took her into his arms without a word. Before Trixie could voice a protest, he kissed her, long and hard, stealing the breath right out of her body. Then he stood back and held his hands on her arms, his eyes bright with hope and longing.

"Stay awhile, Tricia Maria," he said, his breath ragged from the effect of the kiss. "Stay and see for yourself all of the good we're doing here. You owe me that much at least, before you decide what to do about this place."

"Is that why you kissed me?" she asked, her heart pumping, her voice raw with pain.

Logan's mouth came close to hers again. "No, I kissed you because I wanted to, because I couldn't stop myself. But I'm asking you to stay because I intend to fight you on this. I won't let you sell this place without at least putting up a good struggle. You said you'd consider everything and take in all the facts before you made a choice."

"I did say that," she admitted, thinking he was one smooth operator. "And I can't make an informed decision without seeing how this place operates."

He leaned close again, his breath fanning her face. "Then you'll stay?"

She swallowed back the fear coursing through her system. Somehow she knew her answer would change both of their lives. "Yes, I'll stay," she said, her gaze holding his.

"Fair enough."

Logan let her go then, turning to get away from the overpowering urge to pull her back into his arms. He hoped he'd done the right thing by asking her to remain here for a while. He didn't really have any other choice. Somehow, he had to make Trixie see that this place could make a difference, not just in the lives of all of those children, but in her own life, also.

He would do that much at least for Brant's sake.

Even if it meant having to tell Trixie the truth at last.

Chapter Four

"Mother, I've made my decision. I'm only going to stay a few days, so don't worry." Trixie tried once again to convince her mother that she wasn't being impulsive, then listened as Pamela's shrill words shot through the phone line.

"Well, I am worried, young lady," Pamela said with an impatient huff. "You have no business hanging around with that…that field hand."

"Logan is the foreman of this ranch," Trixie reminded her mother, anger causing her to grind the words out. "He's very capable of showing me what's going on here."

"Oh, he's capable, all right. Apparently you've forgotten just exactly what that man is capable of doing."

Trixie closed her eyes, willing herself to stay calm. They'd had this argument before. Pamela did not believe Logan Maxwell was good enough to even speak to her daughter, therefore she couldn't dare acknowledge that he'd done much more, without laying the blame at his feet completely.

"No, Mother, I haven't forgotten anything about Logan. But I'm asking you to trust me on this. I'm not here to stir up things with Logan again. I'm here to make a decision—an important decision—regarding what to do about this ranch."

"Sell it!" Pamela shouted. "It's that simple, Trixie. Harlan has left it up to you, and that's what needs to be done. No decision necessary."

"I disagree, Mother," Trixie replied, her tone firm and controlled in spite of her trembling hand holding the phone. "Since neither the lawyers nor you told me the whole truth about this situation, I'm now forced to investigate things for myself. And that means I have to stay here longer than I'd planned."

Trixie had already called her office and her assistant was prepared to cover matters there. She also had her client list with her, so she could handle any emergencies that came up, if necessary.

"Everything is under control," she told her mother. *Except my heart and your temper,* Trixie thought.

"And what about your engagement party?"

"I'll be back in Dallas in plenty of time to tie up the loose ends for the party."

"You have obligations, Trixie. It's expected—"

"I know, I know," Trixie interrupted. "People will talk and think the worst, and you might miss an opportunity to have your picture in the society pages."

A long sigh. "Tricia Maria, that was low and uncalled for."

"Mother, I'm sorry. Just let me do what has to be done and I'll be home at the end of the week."

"I don't like this."

"You'll get over it."

"Well, I didn't get over it the first time."

Trixie sat silent for a minute, counting to ten until the sting of her mother's deliberate reminder had passed, then said, "No, Mother, neither of us did. And that's something you'll never let me forget, isn't it?"

Realizing she'd been cruel, Pamela tried to make amends. "Darling, I just want you to be happy. And Rad is such a wonderful man. I just want you home, to try on your gown for the party and to help me get all of this organized. You know I've reserved the entire country club, and of course I've invited so many people. Why, I've hired a firm just to address and mail out the invitations, and then I've got the caterers and the florists to deal with. I could really use your help, since this is all for you, anyway."

Automatically forgiving her mother's barbs and ignoring the excited pitch of Pamela's line of conversation, Trixie replied, "You'll do a great job on the party. You've always been one of the best hostesses in Dallas, whether it's for me or anyone else. And I promise I'll be there soon."

The compliment soothed Pamela's fragile ego enough that she gave in. "Oh, all right. Just shed yourself of that place, once and for all, so you can get on with your life."

Trixie hung up, wondering if Pamela had a clue as to what her daughter really wanted out of life. For years now, Trixie had let her mother steer the reins of her existence. And Pamela had taken full advantage of Trixie's disinterest, guiding her to what she believed to be all the right places and all the best people. Trixie had allowed it out of guilt, mostly, and because she herself didn't have the strength or the ambition to really care.

Now, however, Trixie felt the tides of her future changing. It had taken her father's death to cause her to see the light. She'd missed out on so much; she could have been here, by his side, helping him to realize his dream. It was such a big, lofty dream, yet with such a simple concept. He wanted to help others; he wanted to be fair and good and kind and nurturing. And Brant Dunaway had been all of those things. Too late, Trixie saw that now.

Now she was ready to take charge, to make her own decisions, to take a chance. She'd lived in fear over the past eight years, allowing her domineering mother to call the shots. Now, after discovering a whole new side to the father she'd lost touch with, she was willing to go on faith.

But what if she made another mistake?

A knock at her bedroom door brought her head up. Too late to worry about that now. She'd agreed to stay. She wouldn't go back on that promise, no matter how much her doubt nagged at her, right along with her mother, to go back home.

She opened the door to find Logan standing in the upstairs hallway, his hat in his hand, his feet braced apart as he stared down at her. Giving her a quick once-over, he said, "Didn't you bring any working outfits?"

Looking down at her short-sleeved, flower-embroidered blue cotton shirt and matching walking shorts, Trixie shrugged. "Sorry, I didn't bring the proper ranch hand attire. Any suggestions?"

Logan squinted, then made a face. "Well, it ain't what you're wearing, that's for sure."

Trixie frowned. What she was wearing consisted of the best in designer casual wear. "Should I change?"

He snorted, then dragged her out into the hallway with a hand encircling her wrist. "What, into something even more ridiculous than that? No, I kinda like it, even though it's way too fancy for slopping hogs."

Trixie pulled back, her eyes going wide. "Slopping hogs? I'm here to *observe,* Logan. I don't plan on getting up close and personal with any farm animals."

He urged her on ahead of him, his cowboy boots clicking on the planked landing. "Oh, and how are you going to get a feel for this operation if you don't get some hands-on experience?"

Not liking the glee in his tone, Trixie cast a glance at him over her shoulder. If he thought she was going to do physical labor, he was in for a big surprise. "Can't I just watch and still get a feel?"

"Better to get down-and-dirty," he said, his grin telling her that he planned to make her time here a real learning experience.

"You're doing this on purpose," she chided as they marched down the open, planked stairway. "Is this your way of getting revenge on me?"

"Maybe," he readily admitted as they reached the long, spacious Western-style den. "Of course, if I wanted to really chap your hide, I could just kiss you again."

The minute he said it, the teasing light went out of his eyes to be replaced with something deeper and much more intimate. Maybe he was remembering that kiss they'd shared last night in the tack room. It had certainly caused her to remember other kisses and other such teasing conversations.

But since she'd just assured her mother that nothing was stirring between Logan and her, she felt obligated to fight him off. "I'll take the pigs," she retorted, half serious, half afraid he'd really kiss her again, just as punishment.

Logan shook his head, his dark eyes flashing. "Now, that sure makes me feel good about my kissing abilities." Then he turned completely serious again. "Maybe we should make a pact, though—to keep this strictly business."

Trixie saw the brief flash of need warming his dark eyes. Nodding her head, she said, "Good idea. Just show me the ranch, Logan, and I'll make a decision by the end of the week. Then I'll be out of your hair one way or another."

Wanting confirmation, he asked, "So does that mean if you decide to keep the place, you'll give me complete control on how to run it?"

"That depends," she replied. She hadn't thought that far ahead. If she kept the ranch, she'd have to put in an occasional appearance, to make sure the operation was run according to Brant's wishes. That could prove to be very awkward, especially if he tried to kiss her every time they were alone.

"On what?" Logan asked, his gaze direct and questioning.

Hoping to keep things light for now, she retorted, "On whether you make me slop pigs or not."

Logan managed a smile as he watched her move

through the den to the kitchen. One week. One week of torment and torture, one week of having her near, and knowing she had to go back to her world and the man she'd pledged to marry. One week to convince her that she couldn't sell out her heritage. One week to show Tricia Maria Dunaway that she shouldn't sell out, or sell herself short, either. She could do this; she could gain a lot from this ranch. If she was willing to give a little.

And…he could do this. He could do what he had to do to keep this ranch, and his secrets, intact.

But as he watched her now, standing there in her expensive, baby blue ensemble, sipping coffee like a princess as she looked out over the blossoming dawn, Logan knew being with Trixie again would be one of the hardest things he'd ever had to suffer through.

Trixie looked at him then, her blue eyes a perfect match to her fashionable outfit, her cool attitude a perfect example of his notion of all she represented. He had no way of knowing she was a bundle of nerves and that sweat moistened the crisp cotton of her button-up blouse. He had no way of knowing that she was thinking this would be one of the hardest weeks of her life.

"Does Logan make you all work this hard every day?" Trixie asked Marco a couple of hours later.

They stood inside the hog pen, filling a trough with fresh water for the many sows and what looked like thousands of squealing, pink-nosed piglets. In spite of the chaos of animals and teenagers, the place was neat and tidy. The tightly wired fences stretched in symmetric order across the expanse of the paddock, and the animals looked healthy and well fed, their stalls full of fresh hay and clean, cool water.

Trixie only hoped she hadn't mixed up too many piglets when they'd moved the babies and cleaned the stalls earlier. How was she supposed to know which pig went with which sow, anyway? "That man put me in here on purpose. Well, we'll show him, huh, Marco?" That is, if she hadn't orphaned some poor piglet already.

Marco grinned, his black eyes squinting together as he stared up at his new blond-haired friend. "We call him the pigmeister," he said, his words meant for her ears only. "Mr. Logan wants us to learn responsibility," he added, his tone changing to somber as he reconsidered calling his boss/foster parent a derogatory name.

Trixie smiled down at the youngster. He was really sweet, if not somewhat street-wise. As were all of the half dozen children staying here. They ranged in age from sixteen to seven, from what she could tell. Kind of a patchwork family of personalities. And each one had a story to tell. Being a captive audience, she'd listened all morning, her heart opening with each child's tale.

Abusive parents or no parents at all, truancy charges, and some more severe charges, such as petty theft and robbery, colored each story and quickly, effectively turned her apathy into sympathy. These children needed some firm guidance in their young lives. She was proud of her father, and Logan, for providing it.

Now, she grinned back at Marco. "Mr. Logan

seems like a tough taskmaster to me, but I guess it builds character, huh?''

''That's what he tells us when we whine,'' Marco said, giggling as several thirsty sows bumped each other to get to the fresh, cool water. ''Only, Miss Trixie, we don't have to work all day long. As long as we do our assigned chores and attend the Bible study classes, we get free time each day.''

''Great,'' Trixie replied, the sweat beading on her forehead making her wish she had some free time right about now. She was wilted and sweaty, not socialite material at all. ''And what do you and your friends do for fun?''

''We head down to the swimming hole,'' Marco said before running away to take care of more important pig business.

''That sounds like heaven,'' Trixie said to a pink-eyed sow who wanted first dibs on the water supply. Trixie obligingly moved out of the six-hundred pound animal's path, her eyes scanning the pen for Logan. He'd pushed her through the gates, told her to follow Marco's instructions, then had conveniently left.

As she stood there, wondering what the sharply dressed, sharp-minded women of the Metroplex Marketing Professionals would think of her now, she had to laugh. Right this very minute she didn't care what anyone thought. She was dirty and smelly and sweaty, and her white leather sandals would never be the same, but it felt kind of good to be back out in the thick of things—as long as she watched where she stepped.

Shaking her head, she grinned down at the thirsty

sows. "Hold on, ladies, there's plenty of water for everyone."

"You're having way too much fun," Logan said from behind her, echoing her thoughts precisely.

Her grin turned into a grimace as the wind shifted. Giving him a level, daring look, she said, "Did you expect me to burst into tears and beg you to come in here and rescue me?"

"That would have been the highlight of my day," he said as he stepped through the gate and stalked toward her, a look of grudging admiration on his face. He should have known she'd rather die than give in to him. Trixie had always enjoyed a good challenge. Well, he wasn't quite finished with her just yet. "Looks like you've done a passable job here. Ready to move on to worming sheep?"

Trixie turned off the water hose, then stared across the trough at him. "You're kidding, right?"

"Nope. Has to be done, and as always, we could use an extra hand. You get your choice of which end you want to hold, though."

Her groan echoed out over the squeals and grunts of the hogs and pigs. "Logan, need I remind you that I'm still officially your boss? I think I'd just like a shower, then a tour of the ranch and a thorough report on the operation. And I think you've had enough fun at my expense for one day."

He watched her, his gaze rich with an unreadable emotion before he became glib again. "Testy, aren't you? What's the matter, Tricia Maria, break a nail or something?"

Swaying against the bumps of the sows, Trixie glared over at him. "Okay, I've had enough. I did what you asked—I hung out in the pig pen. And I don't mind lending a hand, but I won't stand around and take orders from you just so you can enjoy watching me make a fool of myself.''

Logan quit smiling then, his expression hardening. "Why not? You certainly made me look like a fool all those years ago."

"Oh, is that what this is all about?" she asked, her hands on her hips as she leaned toward him. "You weren't the only one hurt by our brief encounter, Logan. I certainly paid a high price for my one indiscretion."

He inched closer, nudged by grunting snouts. "Oh, did you, now? Funny, I don't see it that way. You seemed to have bounced back pretty quickly, from what I've heard."

"And just what did you hear?" she asked, her breath stopping. Was he suspicious, or just being cruel?

"Your daddy kept tabs on you, Trixie. College, parties, the good life. You picked right up where you left off." He turned quiet, his eyes scanning her face. "I was just…a minor distraction while you slummed with the ranch hands."

His words hurt more than she'd allow him to see. Coming toward him, she tried to pass by, but his hand on her arm and the many grunting sows urging her forward only brought her straight into his arms. Trying to steady her, Logan held her with both hands now.

She looked up into a set of eyes as rich and deep and centered as the mountains behind them. "Is that really how you see me, Logan? As some socialite who used you, then dumped you?"

"Didn't you?"

Tears pricked at her eyes, but she refused to show him her pain. And she certainly couldn't tell him the truth. "How can you even think that? I didn't have any other choice. I had to go back to Dallas."

"Did you really? I think you had several choices, Trixie."

"What do you mean?" she asked, her voice a whisper on the wind, her whole body tense.

Logan stared down at her, his eyes softening only for a minute, his expression changing from harsh to forgiving as he lowered his hands to her back. She waited, knowing he wanted to say something, knowing he needed to tell her what was in his heart.

And then a big, greedy sow came barreling toward the fresh water, her pink eyes daring Trixie to stand in her way. Too late, Trixie and Logan heard the warning cries and high-pitched laughter coming from the young helpers.

"Look out, Miss Trixie," Marco called, clapping his hands together.

Trixie's gaze moved from Logan's face to the animal bearing down on her. Too late.

The sow charged into Trixie's legs like an angry steer plowing into a rodeo clown, taking Trixie completely by surprise. With a gasp of shock, Trixie lost her balance and since she was still holding onto Logan, pulled him right along with her as she stumbled back against the cold, sharp metal of the trough.

And toppled right back into the water.

Sows grunted and squealed, scattering in the mud

as water splashed out over the trough's edge. Logan had no choice but to hold on and enjoy the fall, since Trixie's first reaction was to reach out for him in an effort to save herself.

He landed right smack beside her, laughing as she came up out of the water spitting and snarling.

"Oh, this is all your fault," she said, her face and hair wet and dripping. "Are you satisfied now, Logan Maxwell?"

Logan sat back in the cold water. Then reaching out to steady her, he hauled her close, his gaze sweeping her face. "No, not nearly enough," he admitted on a low growl.

Trixie saw the heat in his expression and felt that same heat pouring through her system. But she couldn't allow him to get too close, not when he obviously resented her so much. "Let me go, Logan," she pleaded, a catch in her voice.

That plea brought Logan quickly to his senses. He let go of her and stood up so fast he almost toppled over the side. Then he offered her a hand. "Sorry. For a minute there, I forgot that things have changed. It won't happen again."

Trixie watched him while the children laughed and gathered around them, and she took all the chaos as an opportunity to regain her composure along with her balance. No matter how good she felt being in his arms, no matter how much she longed to kiss him again, she had to remember that things *had* changed for them. She was engaged to a wonderful, caring man, and Logan…well, Logan had his life here at the ranch. It wouldn't do for her to get caught up in some sentimental fantasy from the past.

After all, she had given up on Logan a long time ago. And with all the history between them, with her one big secret glaring her in the face each time she looked at Logan, things could only go from bad to worse. No, the best thing she could do was to make a decision about this ranch—soon—before she again did something she would regret.

His face blank, Logan helped her out of the trough, then said, "I'll drive you back to the lodge. Get changed, and I'll give you a tour of the place, then we'll get serious about this."

"Okay." She nodded, avoiding the look of regret she saw clearly on his face. Letting him guide her out of the maze of sows, piglets and young people, she looked straight ahead, ashamed and embarrassed and afraid of all the old emotions that had surfaced between them.

That's when she saw little Caleb running across the yard, his youthful face bright with animation, his deep blue eyes lighting up like the sky at dawn.

"Daddy, Daddy, I saw what happened. That was so funny! Was it cold? Did that big sow bite you?"

Logan's gaze shot over to Trixie, a look of guilt and defiance coloring his expression. She stopped, her heart dropping to her feet right along with the water dripping off her body.

Daddy. Caleb had called Logan Daddy. Oh, Lord, was Logan married, then? Was that what he'd been trying to tell her? She couldn't speak. She could only stare over at him and wonder why with all this talk and action regarding kissing, he hadn't even bothered to tell her he had a wife and a son.

Then she remembered, Logan didn't owe her any

explanations. Because she hadn't bothered to tell him that she'd borne his child so long ago.

Finding out that he had obviously gone on with his life so soon after only served as a brutal reminder—he could never know of her deceit. Her secret would have to remain intact, right along with any feelings she might still have for him. She'd have to, once again, bury her hopes. Because she belonged to another man now, and he belonged to another woman.

And a precious little boy.

Chapter Five

Trixie heard the pounding on her bedroom door the minute she stepped out of the shower. She knew it was Logan. She knew because she'd left the paddocks to run all the way to the lodge, then she'd stood in a hot shower, letting the water fall over her body, letting her tears fall at last, as she'd screamed a silent scream of longing and regret. The memory of Logan's kiss, of his arms holding her, was too much to bear now that she knew he had a family of his own. What kind of game was he playing with her, anyway? Was this his way of punishing her?

She didn't know why it hurt so much. After all, Logan deserved some happiness, and so did she. And the fact that they'd both found it with other people should make her feel better instead of worse. Maybe she was just jealous. Jealous because Logan had a child and she…she'd allowed their child to slip away.

She thought of little Caleb, and wondered how she'd missed it before. The same thick, wispy hair.

The same facial features and body shape. Everything about the child looked like Logan, now that she put it together.

Except his eyes. Caleb had deep blue eyes, while Logan's were a beautiful chocolate brown. She supposed the blue came from the mother's side. And, where was that mother? What was going on?

She started crying all over again as she dressed hurriedly.

Trying to be rational, she reminded herself she'd just lost her father. No wonder this emptiness felt like a gaping hole that would never be filled again. She was still so grief-stricken, it was only natural to feel lonely and depressed and resentful. This would pass. Once she got back to Dallas, back to Rad and their plans together, this ache would surely go away.

The intense knocking at her door, however, didn't go away. "Trixie, let me in. We need to talk."

"Hold on," she managed to say, her voice raw, her words stiff and forced.

Grabbing a floral print sundress, she threw it over her underwear and slip, then ran a brush through her wet hair. Taking a minute, she willed herself to calm down, remembering all the etiquette coaching her Miss Manners mother had drilled into her over the years. Pamela had taught her to always remain a lady, even in the most critical times. For once she had to agree with her mother. She did not want Logan to see her like this. Her hands were still trembling, though, as she opened the door.

Logan filled the room with a caged presence, still in his own wet clothes, his expression guarded and worried. Bringing up a hand, then dropping it to his side, he said, "Ah, you've been crying. Trixie, I'm sorry. I didn't mean for you to find out this way—"

She halted him with a hand in the air. "It's all right. I'm glad for you, Logan. Really I am."

Surprised, he stopped his pacing. "What?"

She looked up at him, a fresh batch of tears welling in her red-rimmed eyes. "I don't know why you didn't trust me enough to tell me that you're married and have a child, but I understand how awkward this is for you."

Seeing the relief washing over his face, she stammered on, "And...I'd really like to meet your wife. Silly, why didn't you introduce us already? Caleb is such a beautiful little boy." Her voice broke in spite of the cheery smile she tossed out at him. "I'm sure his mother is just as beautiful."

Logan reached out a hand to wipe a single teardrop from her cheek. "She is," he said, his words hushed and choked. "But Trixie, there's something you need to know."

Trixie swallowed back another sob, the touch of his finger on her skin like a healing balm. Not wanting him to pity her, or be nice to her, she said, "What's that?"

Logan stood there, staring down at her, as if weighing just how much he should tell her. "I'm...I'm not married anymore."

She gazed up at him, her own relief so strong she almost fell into his arms. "You're not?"

Logan dropped his hand away from her face to stand back at a safe distance. "No. The marriage ended a long time ago. Actually, it ended before it really had a chance to begin."

Concern replaced the joy in her heart. But relief lightened her load considerably. "What happened? Did you make her slop pigs?"

The attempt at humor brought a wry smile to his face. "No, she liked living here. Ranch life agreed with her, but unfortunately, I didn't." He lowered his head, regret evident in his hushed words. "I...I married her straight into my first year of college...and I didn't really appreciate her or love her enough to make it stick."

Trixie nodded her understanding. He'd obviously married someone else right after she'd left him. She could see the pain in his eyes. It mirrored the pain in her own heart. "Where is she now?"

"Back in Little Rock, remarried and happy with a new baby, last I heard."

She had to wonder, had to voice it. "And...you got custody of Caleb?"

His head came up then. He hesitated, then slowly nodded. "Yeah. This ranch is the only home he's ever known. He was real young when...when all of this happened. He doesn't know his mother at all."

"You told me his mother abandoned him," she reminded him gently, her heart going out to both Logan and his son.

"She did," he said, a darkness moving across his expression. "She left...not too long after he was born."

Trixie closed her eyes, afraid he'd see the guilt of what she considered her own abandonment of their child written there. "Does she ever see him now?"

He gave her a direct look. "No." The harshness of

the one word startled Trixie. But not as much as the simmering rage she saw in his eyes.

Sensing the evasiveness in his answer, she decided not to press him anymore about something so devastating. He was obviously still shaken, still angry, about the whole thing. This at least explained some of the bitterness she'd sensed in him.

The Logan she remembered rarely opened up; she should be glad she'd gotten this far with him. And to think, he'd managed to raise his child on his own, here on the ranch with his mother's help. Trixie's respect for him went up another notch. "Thank you for telling me the truth."

His head came up then, a look of disgust crossing his face. "The truth hurts, sweetheart. You should know that better than anybody."

Confused, she felt as if he could see straight into her heart. "I do, Logan. I do." Closing her eyes for a minute, she added, "But you're so lucky."

He grunted. "Oh, and how's that?"

Awe colored her words. "You have a beautiful child. You have a son. That's such a wonderful gift."

When she opened her eyes, the look he gave her made her take a step back. It was a mixture of pain and regret, and something else…anger. But instead of being directed toward his ex-wife, this anger centered on Trixie herself. She could feel it; could see it in his whole stance, in the way he curled his fists at his side.

"Logan?"

He backed out the door before she could recover, then pivoted in the hallway to give her a parting look.

"Well, you'll be married soon yourself. Maybe you'll have a whole passle of kids."

"Rad wants to wait awhile," she blurted out, then instantly regretted it after Logan snorted and glared at her.

A smirk followed the snort. "Good idea. Keep it all neat and tidy. A workable plan where you can pencil them in when it's convenient."

"Logan, Rad isn't that way," she said, wanting to defend the man she'd promised to marry, even though Logan had summed him up pretty accurately. "He just knows what he wants out of life."

Logan stepped back into the room then, his eyes meeting hers, his words whispering across her skin. "And do you? Do you know what you want out of life, Tricia Maria?"

Right now she wanted him to take her in his arms and hold her, but she knew that was wrong. And right now, with the mood he was in, she didn't think he'd be willing to let her cry on his shoulder.

"Yes, I do," she said, bobbing her head. "I just want to be happy."

He stood silent, weighing the anguish in her words, his anger and resentment misting around him like a heavy fog. "And this Rad...he's the man to make you happy?"

She didn't miss the hint of a dare in his question.

"I think so," she replied, her arms wrapped across her chest defensively.

At least, that's what everyone back home kept telling her, and that's what she kept telling herself. Thinking about it now, she felt a certain contentment, a certain comfort in knowing she had Rad to turn to.

But she had to admit, her feelings for Rad were completely different from what she'd once felt for Logan.

But then, *that* had been so strong, so swift, so all consuming, she still held the scars from their brief encounter. Better to settle for contentment, rather than something so burning hot it felt like lightning shooting through her system. And scorched just as badly.

Logan picked up on her doubts like a wild mustang sniffing the wind.

He leaned close again, his dark eyes glowing with this new, intriguing knowledge. "Take it from someone who's been there, honey. You'd better be sure." With that, he turned, his boots clicking as he stalked out of the room. "I'm going to change, then I'll be downstairs waiting. Take your time."

Trixie had the distinct feeling he was referring to more than her getting dressed. Did Logan want her to take her time in making the right decision? Or did he just want more time before she pledged her heart to another man?

"'Reproach hath broken my heart, and I am full of heaviness, and I looked for some to take pity, but there was none, and for comforters, but I found none.'"

Logan finished reading the verse from Proverbs, then looked up at the faces of the teenagers and children listening to him. For a long while he simply sat there underneath the old oak tree where they held daily Bible discussions when the weather was nice, his thoughts automatically going out to Trixie.

He'd treated her badly since the little revelation in the pig paddock, dragging her around the ranch, his mood snarly and tight-lipped, his answers to her many questions clipped and precise. Sure, he'd seen the pain, the hurt in her blue eyes, but he didn't care. No, she'd caused him too much suffering for him to feel any compassion, any comfort, toward her.

But had he been wrong all this time?

Did she suffer from a broken heart, the same way he did? Up until now, he'd often wondered if she even had a heart. But something in the way she'd cried, something in the fresh-faced little girl he'd seen today, had brought a measure of compassion to his own hardened heart. Maybe he'd been unfair to her all of these years, blaming her for something she had no control over, blaming her for his own preconceived notions about the girl he'd known so briefly, yet so intimately. Brant had tried to tell him, had defended his daughter again and again, but Logan had never been listening, really. Maybe because he wanted to think the worst of Trixie, maybe because it was just easier that way to accept that she would never be his.

He couldn't continue blaming Trixie, though, when he'd played such a big part in all of this himself. No, Trixie had had no other choice back then. Knowing her formidable mother from his many discussions of Pamela with Brant, Logan could understand the powerhouse of force Trixie had faced. No wonder she'd gone away and never tried to reach out to him again, in spite of their promises and pledges to each other in the heat of the moment.

Today, today, he'd seen that same Trixie who'd pledged her love to him, standing there in her sundress, her hair wet and smelling like summer rain, her eyes as blue as the September sky coloring the changing leaves. He'd seen the young girl, confused and afraid, reaching out to someone, something she could cling to and hold close for comfort. And he'd pushed her away, once again blaming her for things that had happened long ago when they were both young and impassioned. Why had he been so bitter all these years?

"Daddy, why do you look so sad?" Caleb asked from his perch on a gnarled oak root. "Finish talking, Daddy. It's 'bout time for supper."

"Sorry, pal," Logan said, regaining some of his composure as he stared down at his son. "Guess I got lost in thought there for a minute."

"I never been lost in thought," Caleb answered, his grin endearing. "Is it scary?"

Logan smiled, amazed at the simplicity children always brought to the complexities of life. "It sure can be, son," he said truthfully. "Sometimes, you know, we get so caught up in thinking about things, we stay all mad and pouting and we forget to take action to make things change."

Samantha Webster, the youth counselor Brant had saved from the streets, nodded her head, her intricately braided hair shifting gracefully over her dark shoulders. "Action speaks louder than words."

"Right," Logan agreed, "and I do believe that's what this particular passage of the Bible is saying." At the confused looks on the young faces before him, he added, "Here is a person looking for someone to forgive him. He's sad, he's lonely, he's afraid, but no one wants to be bothered with his problems. So they turn away. How they act speaks louder than any words they might say.''

"They acted bad?'' Marco asked, his big eyes widening as he waited for an answer.

Logan nodded, thinking this lesson could sure apply to him. "They didn't want to offer this person their help or their understanding.''

"That ain't nice,'' Caleb admonished, swiping his hand across his nose for emphasis.

"Sure isn't,'' Samantha readily agreed, her chocolate-colored eyes lighting up as she smiled down at Caleb. "I've felt that way before myself, before Mr. Brant brought me here and taught me about loving other people. If he hadn't reached out to me and shown me some comfort, I wouldn't have changed my life. But I finished high school with honors and went on to college, thanks to him. If he hadn't taken action with me, I wouldn't be here today, that's for sure.''

"And you love us now, don't you?'' Caleb asked the young woman.

"I sure do.'' Just to prove her point, Samantha grabbed the boy up and tickled him, causing him to squeal out in pleasure.

Logan watched, his own heart opening like a long-dormant flower. Caleb didn't care where Samantha had come from; he just knew she was his friend and teacher. His son was special that way. The little boy didn't have a mean bone in his body. His innocence always brought a sense of awe to Logan and a sense of fierce protection. Because he'd never known his own father, Logan had vowed Caleb would always be

a part of his life, and he a part of his son's. He wasn't
about to let anybody change that.

And that included Tricia Maria Dunaway. Okay, so
maybe he'd been a little hard on her, but he still had
a right to fight for this ranch and his son's future.
And he'd do best to focus on his own obligations,
rather than worrying about Trixie's welfare. She had
old money and a new, powerful husband-to-be to take
care of her. As he watched his son now, he knew he
didn't have to be reminded of what was at stake here.
Caleb would always be his first concern.

But as he ended the lesson, he prayed for compassion regarding Trixie. He would try really hard to give
her the benefit of the doubt. Maybe she wasn't all
bad; maybe she'd had her own reasons for leaving
him behind so long ago. Being around her had certainly reminded him of the good in her, and today
he'd seen that good in her tears and her open honesty.

But being around her had also reminded him of
how much he'd once loved her. That love had turned
out to be a huge mistake. Remembering that, he asked
God for guidance. And he prayed that one day the
truth would at last be told between Trixie and him.
Maybe that would be the only way to find true compassion. Maybe that would be the only way to heal
the burden of his own heavy heart.

From the kitchen window, Trixie watched as Logan
finished the hour of Bible study. The gentle, patient
man she saw out there now was a far cry from the
rude, brusque man who'd reluctantly escorted her
around the ranch for the past few hours. She'd real-

ized over the course of the afternoon that Logan was mad at women in general, and especially her.

But how could he continue blaming her for what had happened, or what had not happened between them? True, she'd promised to spend eternity with him. She'd wanted nothing more than to stay here on the ranch and marry him. That had been their dream; their promise. But then, all of that changed when Brant found out just how far they'd taken things between them.

She'd been whisked away, and then she'd found out she was carrying his child. How many times had she thought about calling him, telling him the truth? How many times had she dreamed of them being together here with their child? But she couldn't tell Logan about any of her foolish dreams. And if anyone had a right to be bitter, it was Trixie.

He'd never even bothered coming after her. He'd just let her go, without a word between them. Well, she was here now. Maybe it was time for words, lots of words. Maybe if they could sit down and talk this through, they'd both find some sort of peace at last.

A rich golden dusk settled over the hills and valleys behind him, while he read and talked quietly to the children, his deep voice carrying out over the evening breeze. Again she was struck by his physical attractiveness. He looked right at home, sitting there on the ground in his Levi's and cotton shirt, fresh from an evening shower after a long day's work, his dark hair curling up in the wind, the laugh lines at his eyes crinkling whenever he stressed an important point, or cracked a joke.

It bothered her that she would even compare this

man to Rad. But she couldn't help herself. Rad was clean-cut to a fault, always dressed in the finest and latest that money could buy, a picture-perfect version of the successful, up-and-coming associate of one of the oldest law firms in Dallas, a firm where his father just happened to be a senior partner.

"A perfect companion, a perfect gentleman," Pamela always told her friends. "Meant for my Trixie."

Funny, Trixie thought now. She'd once believed the man sitting out underneath that tree had been meant for her. Funny how her life had changed so much; how her attitude had changed so much. Watching Logan with his son only made her memories of their time together more poignant. Somewhere out there a child walked around with Logan's features and personality, mixed with her own.

Somewhere.

Maybe it was too late for them to find any peace, but it surely wasn't too late for her to continue her father's work here. Logan had at least opened up on that subject.

Brant had had big plans, but he'd died before he could finish them. He wanted to expand the ranch into a year-round school for underprivileged children, complete with certified teachers and the best in educational facilities. That would mean building a small school and more dorms; that would also mean more money needed and lots of hard work.

Could she do that? Trixie wondered now. Could she commit herself to such a lofty task, all the while knowing she'd have to work closely with Logan?

"You can go out there and join them," Gayle said

from her spot near the stove, her tone implying Trixie could use a good dose of gospel.

"No, I'll just stay in here with you, if you don't mind," Trixie replied, thinking she'd just have to weigh all of her options and make the right decision. Starting with winning over Logan's taciturn mother. "I wouldn't want to interrupt. Logan is so good with those kids."

Gayle kept stirring the pot of red beans and rice. "Logan is a good man."

"I know that," Trixie said, coming to stand by the older woman. "I've always known that, I think."

Gayle looked over at her, her hostile gaze sweeping over Trixie's face. "But not good enough for the likes of you, right?"

Startled by the woman's insistent hostility, Trixie asked, "What does that mean?"

Gayle shrugged, then checked the clock. "It means that you hurt my son a long time ago and that I'm worried you might do the same thing again."

Trixie waited a minute, forming her answer carefully. It wouldn't do for Gayle to become even more suspicious of her motives. "I never meant to hurt Logan. I cared about him, probably too much. And…we were very young."

"And foolish," Gayle admitted, her eyes softening a bit. "My son is as much to blame as you. I know that, and we've talked about his part in your little fling."

"It wasn't just a fling," Trixie said, wanting Gayle to understand that she had not taken her one night with Logan lightly. "I really cared about him, and I think he cared about me. But…we got carried away and then…circumstances pulled us apart.''

''Right.'' The coldness resurfaced in Gayle's eyes. ''Such as…you wanted a better life, with all the glamour and wealth your grandfather's oil money could provide. So you left in a great rush.''

Angry and tired, Trixie countered, ''Did you really expect my father to allow me any other choice?''

Gayle had the decency to look embarrassed. ''No, I know Brant was furious with both of you. I guess he did the only thing he could do. He sent you away. And of course, you did have your mother to deal with.''

Trixie nodded, the memories of her shame still like a sharp knife in her heart. ''I was so embarrassed and confused. My mother preached to me day and night about my sin, until she had me convinced of my unworthiness.'' She reached out a hand to touch Gayle's arm. ''But I did care about Logan.''

Gayle stared hard at her, her expression wavering only a fraction. ''Enough to beg your father to keep Logan on here.'' It was a flat statement, but a true one.

''Yes.'' Trixie lowered her head, wishing Brant were here himself so she could talk to him. ''I didn't want you or Logan to have to find work somewhere else.''

Gayle reached out a hand to pat Trixie's arm. ''I know how much you cared about my son, Tricia Maria. Logan cared about you, too. Why, you two were inseparable back then. Brant and I should have seen it coming, but, well…this place gets the best of you sometimes. But, I do appreciate your efforts toward calming your father down. Logan needed his job back then, just as he does now. I'm just worried…that's all. Seems like I've always got something to worry over.''

Trixie saw the concern in the dark shadows of fatigue surrounding Gayle's eyes. ''And now, it's about me selling?''

''That and—'' Laughter from the yard brought Gayle's head up. ''Oh, look at me, going on and on about things we can't neither one change. It's time for grub. Want to help me serve the kids out on those two picnic tables?''

''Sure.'' Glad that the woman was at least being somewhat civil to her, Trixie wondered what else Gayle Maxwell wanted to say to her. There was something going on here, some shared bond between mother and son, that Trixie was afraid she wouldn't be able to break.

What were they hiding?

Watching Gayle now, Trixie had a thought. Then, sure she'd hit upon part of the reason for Gayle's reserved attitude, she decided she'd have to ask some questions to find out if she had pinpointed some of the woman's real concerns. The answer was so simple, so obvious, Trixie wondered why she'd never seen it before.

Gayle Maxwell had been in love with her father.

And maybe that was why she'd been acting so strangely. She resented Trixie because now Trixie had the power to take away Gayle's only link with Brant Dunaway.

It was the only explanation.

And it was one more reason for Trixie to weigh

the consequences of her actions very carefully. Saying a silent prayer, she asked God to help her. She had a feeling though, that no matter her decision, someone would wind up on the losing end.

It might be all of the children who needed this sanctuary. It might be Gayle and Logan and little Caleb.

Or it might turn out to be Trixie herself.

She'd lost once, based on other people's decisions. This time, though, the responsibility rested solely on her shoulders.

"I can't bear it alone, Lord," she whispered. "I'm asking for Your help."

For everyone's sake.

Chapter Six

"Granddaddy, what are you doing back here?" Trixie asked the next morning when she came downstairs to find Harlan sitting at the table, eating a hearty breakfast with Logan and Gayle.

He'd left right after the burial service, his old heart broken and heavy from the death of his only son. But Harlan Dunaway always bounced back, and he always looked on the bright side of things. Which is why his smiling face did a lot to boost Trixie's own sagging spirits. She could certainly use some reinforcements right about now.

Hugging him close, she thanked God for small favors. "I'm glad you're back, but why so soon?"

"Came to check up on you, girly," Harlan replied between bites of bacon tucked into a fluffy biscuit. "Your ma's fretting something awful over you being up here, while she's trying to get this engagement shindig organized."

"Good grief." Ignoring the way Logan's gaze

heated her skin, Trixie headed straight for the coffee-pot. She had not had a good night's sleep, and now this. Although she was thrilled to see her lovable grandfather, she didn't like hearing about Pamela's interference. "Tell Mother to stop worrying about me. I'm a grown woman now."

Harlan huffed a grunt at about the same time as Logan.

"Well, I'm glad you both agree on that," Trixie said, her eyes moving from her grandfather's amused face to Logan's stony expression.

"That's what's got her worrying," Harlan said, winking over at Logan.

Trixie saw the look that passed between the two men. Was Harlan warning Logan away from her in his own none-too-tactful way? Would her family ever let her make her own decisions?

Deciding to head him off at the pass, she said, "You're sure in a good mood for a man bringing dire tidings of dread." Purposely turning away from Logan's frowning face, she sat down beside her grandfather and gave him a quick kiss. "But I am glad for your company, and I could use your advice."

Harlan just smiled and chewed. "All I got is time, honey. I'll be happy to help in any way I can."

"What'll you have?" Gayle asked Trixie, her tone quiet and firm, her eyes wary and guarded.

"Just toast," Trixie replied, her gaze still on her grandfather.

Logan grunted again, louder this time, his scowling gaze slamming down on Trixie. "Still eats like a bird."

Harlan's chuckle jiggled his own ample belly.

"Habit, son. Always watching her weight, because of all those beauty pageants her Ma used to force her to enter—ruined her appetite for real food."

Trixie turned up her nose, posing in true beauty queen fashion. She'd hated being put on display back during her teenage years, and she and Pamela had had more than one royal battle when she'd announced to her frantic mother that she was retiring from the pageant circuit. "I won a few, but thankfully those days are over."

Logan's expression bordered on hostile while his searching gaze flickered over her face. "Well, then you don't have to starve yourself anymore to look good, Trixie. Eat something for goodness' sake."

Groaning, Trixie wished she'd stayed upstairs. She was in no mood to argue with the sanctimonious Logan Maxwell, or her playful grandfather. "If you two will quit fussing over me, I'll be perfectly fine. I'm not a big breakfast person."

Harlan shook his head, then chuckled again. "She always was grumpy in the morning."

"Rough night?" Logan asked, his eyes scanning her face. If misery loved company, he hoped she'd been as miserable as he'd been last night. He was beginning to wonder if asking her to stay had been the right idea after all.

Trixie hit him with a scathing glare, the blue in her eyes lighting like a flame's tip. "I've had better."

"None of us has been getting much sleep lately," Gayle said from her chair at the end of the plank table, her work-roughened fingers clutching a white coffee mug. She looked over at Trixie, her meaning evident. "Things are changing around here. First your father's sudden death, and now you…thinking about selling this place. It's all too much, I guess. That's why we're all so ornery.''

Trixie wanted to scream, but Gayle had a point. To smooth things over, she said, ''Yes, it's been hard on all of us. But I promised you both I won't make a hasty decision.'' Then she glanced at Harlan. ''Daddy sure had lots of plans for this place. Big plans. I realize there's a trust fund set up, and that regular donations come in, but I just don't know about the work involved. I could hire a consulting firm, or I could tackle it myself—that is if I decide to keep the ranch.''

Harlan nodded, then took a long swig of coffee. ''I trust you, darling. You'll do what's right.''

Gayle wasn't convinced. Slinging a dry dishrag over her shoulder, she shoved her chair back to go on about her daily business, her expression tight-lipped and unrelenting.

Trying to ignore Gayle's obvious disapproval and distrust, Trixie turned to her grandfather again. ''How long will you be here?''

''Long enough to bring back either you, or a convincing report, to your mother.''

Trixie would like nothing better than to go home, but she still had a lot to deal with and even more emotional trauma to work through. ''I'll be staying a few days longer,'' she said to Harlan.

Her grandfather's eagle eyes moved from her face to Logan's scowl. ''I see.''

Hoping to reassure him that everything was all right, Trixie said, ''Want to go for a ride with Logan and me? He promised we'd take a couple of the horses out, so I can see the rest of the place."

And she really didn't want to be alone with Logan. Last night at supper he'd stared at her so long and hard, she'd felt a permanent imprint, like a brand, burning her skin.

She'd sat there, listening to the banter of the young people, listening to Caleb's infectious giggles, listening to the night sounds and the sounds of harmony and fellowship echoing throughout the cookhouse, only to have Logan remind her that she really didn't belong here in the first place.

And to make matters worse, he kept sending her mixed messages. One minute he was gazing at her like a man obsessed, and the next, well, if looks could kill....

"I'd enjoy that," Harlan agreed, rising up out of his chair, his knowing eyes moving between his granddaughter and Logan. "Provided, of course, Logan can find a mount with enough muscle to hold me."

Logan finally took his gaze away from Trixie long enough to form the makings of a grin. "I think I can manage that, sir."

"I'll be out in a minute," Trixie told the men. "I want to help Gayle with the dishes."

"No need," Gayle rushed to say. "Samantha will send one of the young people to help me after they've finished their meal out in the cookhouse."

"I don't mind," Trixie said, her tone firm, her eyes centered on the other woman. She might not get any answers from Logan, but she intended to corner his mother, at least.

Logan glanced over at his mother, concern apparent on his haggard features. "Is everything all right here?"

Gayle turned to give her son a reassuring look. "It's fine, son. Trixie and I are just getting reacquainted, is all."

Trixie noticed how reluctant he seemed to leave them alone, further confirmation that something wasn't quite right. But after giving her and Gayle a warning look, he left with Harlan, anyway.

Turning to face Gayle, she said, "Why do you hate me so much?"

"I don't," Gayle replied in her own direct way, busying herself with stacking their breakfast dishes in the sink. "I told you, I've got a lot on my mind."

"You miss my father, don't you?"

Gayle's expression softened at the mention of Brant. "Yes, I sure do. This place just ain't the same without him coming down those stairs, shouting for coffee and grits."

Bracing herself, Trixie lifted her head and asked, "Did you…love him?"

Gayle watched Trixie's face for censure, and seeing none, nodded. "Yes…I loved him so very much."

A sad sigh escaped through Trixie's parted lips. "I thought so. I could tell, by the way you say his name, by the way you smile when you're talking about him." Placing a hand on Gayle's arm, she asked, "Did he know how you felt?"

Gayle shook her head, her eyes watering up. "Brant only had eyes for your mother, Tricia Maria. I accepted that long ago, but I stayed here, watching out for him, taking care of him, because…I couldn't imagine doing anything else, going anyplace else.''

Turning Gayle around with a hand on each of the other woman's sagging shoulders, Trixie said, ''Why didn't you ever tell him?''

Gayle sniffed, then reached for a tissue from the box on the windowsill, that one action as telling as the sad frown on her face. ''Oh, I tried, many times. But…so much had happened. He worried about you all the time, but he had to keep his distance. Your mother made it hard for him to hear any news of you. I'd watch him sometimes, late at night, standing out there underneath that great oak. He'd look off in the distance, his coffee cup in his hand. And I knew, I knew he was thinking of her. Always her.''

She gave Trixie a direct, daring look that reminded her of Logan. ''I lost one man to another woman, and I vowed I'd never be second best again. So, Brant and I stayed friends—close, compatible, comfortable. And every night I'd go into my room down here by the kitchen and he'd go up to that big bedroom he'd designed especially for her. I didn't have the guts to push myself on him, and I wouldn't dream of…of doing anything without the sanctity of marriage. It just wouldn't have been right.''

She stopped, seeing the dread and shame covering Trixie's face in a heated rush. ''I'm sorry.''

''It's okay,'' Trixie said, glad Gayle had told her about her special relationship with Brant. ''I agree with you completely.''

Gayle patted her on the hand, admiration showing in her eyes at last. ''It's hard, nowadays, living up to your convictions. There's a lot of temptation in this old world.''

Yes, Trixie thought. And her main one was out there saddling up a horse with her grandfather. Well, Gayle's honesty had opened her eyes to one thing at least. She wouldn't fall back into her old pattern with Logan. They had to behave like rational adults now, for the sake of this ranch and the example they had to uphold for the young people sent here for guidance. Just a hint of scandal could shut this place down, regardless of how she felt about keeping it open.

And, she reminded herself, she was promised to another. She wouldn't do anything to jeopardize her relationship with Rad. It was high time she practiced some of her convictions.

"My father was lucky to have your friendship, Gayle. And your love. Thank you for taking care of him."

"I did the best I could for him," Gayle replied.

"I'm glad we had this talk. It explains a lot to me about why you seemed so worried and resentful toward me. But I do want you to know, I'm also pleased that my father had you here. I'm sure it helped ease some of his loneliness."

Gayle didn't say anything. She only nodded and whirled to stare out the window. Then, her back still turned, she said, "Maybe, then, you can understand why I don't want Logan to spend the rest of his life pining away for you. Don't give him any false hope, Trixie. This time, I do believe it would destroy him for good."

Her heart pounding, Trixie knew what she had to do. Once again she would have to walk away in order to protect Logan and his mother…and what little dignity she had left herself. The decision was an easy one, based on lots of hard lessons.

"I'm not going to give him any false hope, Gayle," she said quietly. "But I am going to give him something else." When Gayle pivoted to her with questioning eyes, she held out a hand to the woman. "I'm going to give him total control over this ranch in my absence."

Gayle's hand flew to her throat. "You…you're not going to sell?"

"No," Trixie said, her smile bittersweet. "Once, long ago, I let go of something very precious, and I've regretted it ever since. I won't let it happen again. So, I'm going to keep the ranch and trust Logan to follow my father's stipulations regarding how things are handled. No, I'm not going to sell."

Tears of relief and joy fell down Gayle's face as she took Trixie's hand in her own. "Oh, Logan will be so glad. You don't know how much this will mean to us."

Just then the screen door burst open and Caleb came running in, his cowboy hat tipped at a rakish angle, his deep blue eyes bright with the unexpected treasure he'd just discovered. "Nana, Nana, I found some baby kittens behind the barn. Wanna come see?"

"*I* sure do," Trixie said, wanting to cry herself for some strange reason.

Maybe because life on this ranch was so much more real, so much more poignant, than the life she'd always known, growing up in Dallas. She'd never been allowed to touch stray cats.

Except, she remembered now with brilliant clarity, once when she'd been around ten, and Brant had come sneaking into the kitchen, holding a finger to his lips and a tiny furry gray creature in his hand. "Look what I found out in the stables. Wanna hold the kitten, Trixiebelle?"

"Yes!" Trixie had leaped from her perch on a breakfast stool, dropping down to rub her hands over the soft, warm fur while her big father knelt and cooed to the frightened little animal. Of course, Pamela had come into the room, promptly breaking up the father-daughter conspiracy.

"Get that thing out of this kitchen, Brant Dunaway," her mother had insisted, a finger pointed to the back door. "You don't know where that cat's been. It's filthy and germy, and I won't have my daughter exposed to it."

And sadly, Trixie thought now, that had set the tone for most of her life.

"Well, come on," Caleb said, bringing her out of the bittersweet flashback. "I know right where they're hidin', but you have to be careful. They scratch." Proudly he held out a hand to show her a spot where he'd been clawed.

"Wait just a minute." Gayle's brief joyous attitude changed immediately back into one of wariness and distrust. "You better get on out there for your morning ride," she reminded Trixie, her arms going around her grandson in a protective, loving gesture.

"I will, after Caleb shows me the kittens," Trixie said, bending down to smile at the little boy. He looked so much like Logan it took her breath away and brought another rush of great pain to her heart.

"I don't think that's a good idea," Gayle insisted as she shoved the boy behind her skirts, her stance guarded and defiant.

Surprised, Trixie stood up to stare over at her. "And why not?"

Gayle sniffed back the last of her happy tears and said, "Because, quite frankly, I don't think Logan wants you around his boy."

Stunned and hurt, Trixie could only stare over at the woman. When Caleb's big curious eyes shifted from his grandmother to Trixie, she backed down. It wouldn't do to upset the little boy by provoking an argument with his stubborn grandmother.

Bending down again, she said in a controlled voice, "Tell you what, Caleb. Since your Daddy is waiting on me, why don't you get that scratch cleaned up and then take Grandmama to see the kittens, and when I get back from my ride I'll peek in on them, okay?"

Caleb let out an exaggerated sigh, then plopped his rickety hat down on the table. "Oh, okay. Know what, Miss Trixie?"

"What, sweetie?"

"If one of 'em's a girl kitten, I'm gonna name her Trixie, after you."

The tears did come then, unbidden and uncensored, but Trixie swallowed them back. Reaching out a hand to touch Caleb's thick tousle of hair, she managed to say, "Thank you. That's very sweet." Then she stood and rushed out the door, gently closing the screen between them.

"What's the matter with Miss Trixie, Nana?" she heard Caleb say.

"Nothing for you to worry about," Gayle replied softly.

When Trixie turned to look back inside, Gayle was hugging her grandson close. Over the child's head, her eyes met Trixie's. And that's when Trixie saw something else there in the other woman's gaze.

Fear.

Because both Trixie and Logan were in rather dark moods, it was left to Harlan to do the talking as the trio walked their horses down the fenced dirt lane that cut through the pastures and hills of the ranch.

Everywhere around them the trees and grasses were slowly changing from green to brown. Soon the surrounding hills and mountains would be radiant with the colors of fall.

To Harlan's way of thinking, however, there was already a chill in the air between these two. They'd just finished surveying most of the acreage, and as the sun climbed to lofty heights, so did his granddaughter's haughty attitude toward the brooding, tight-lipped foreman.

"Fine morning, ain't it?" Harlan said to the wind, since neither of the two young people on either side of him had seemed to notice the golden haze of late September settling over the earth. "Indian summer's here. Then those crisp, cool days of autumn. God's handiwork, children—it always amazes me."

"Right," Logan grunted, his hat slung low over his brow, his back straight in the saddle.

"Beautiful," Trixie replied, her gaze focused on the distant mountains, her mind focused on Gayle's strange behavior back in the kitchen.

"Gonna get hot before the day's out, though," Harlan continued, referring to much more than the weather. Glancing over at Trixie, he said, "And might I add, you look like sunshine yourself in that yellow outfit, Trixiebelle."

"Why, thank you." His compliment brought a measure of triumph to Trixie's hurting heart. In pure defiance of Logan's "work clothes" rule, she'd worn a button-up yellow cotton shirt that had embroidered sunflowers plastered across the bodice, and the matching knee-length shorts with sunflowers rimming the full legs. Let him make fun of that!

He did. "Yeah, she looks like a regular walking garden. Guess we ought to take her over to Brant's sunflower patch and throw her right smack dab in the middle."

"Good idea," Harlan agreed, his chuckle laced with a tad too much cheer. Deciding to change the subject to business only, he said, "Let's see—we've seen the sheep, the cows and pigs, the farm equipment—all of that seems in working order. We've talked about the harvest—corn's just about ready to be pulled, fall produce looks excellent. And the counselors you're hired are doing a great job with the young 'uns. Looks like you've got everything under control, Logan."

"Except who's gonna wind up being my boss," Logan said in a huffy breath, cutting his gaze to Trixie.

Trixie hadn't told him her decision yet. Her mind was in such turmoil she couldn't think straight. And especially with him riding that horse like a born cowboy, making her heart turn all mushy and her breath

stop in her throat. Memories of another time, and this
same man, only added to her misery.

She remembered the first time she'd seen Logan.
She was standing in the stables, fresh off the plane
from Little Rock, petting a mare and her new foal
while she waited for her father to come in from the
pastures. The late-afternoon sun cast a burnished
sheen through the arched gateway, framing the humid
air in a glistening stillness. She looked up to see a
darkened shadow of a man approaching, but the man
certainly wasn't her father. He looked mysterious and
dangerous, his hat slung low over his brow, his jeans
dirty and snug, his eyes...his eyes burning with a
knowing, cynical fire.

A cowboy, home from mending fences, his attitude
as intact and intense as the barbed wire surrounding
the far pastures.

A young socialite, innocent and searching, searching for something, someone, her whole world shattered by her parents' divorce.

Oh, Logan, she thought now, afraid to look at him,
*we were so young, so afraid, so anxious to find some
sense of comfort and peace. We had no way of knowing our whole lives would change that autumn.*

Reminding herself that she'd decided to live by her
convictions, she stopped her horse and called out to
the two men riding up ahead of her. "Granddaddy, I
need to talk to Logan. Do you mind?"

Harlan whirled his sturdy mount around with
expert agility. "Heck, no, honey. Don't mind at all.
'Bout time for my lunch and my nap, anyway. I'll
just go visit your pa's grave for a spell, then head
back to the house." Then he brought his horse close

to her own. "Like I said at breakfast, I'm trusting you to make the right decision. And I know you will."

Trixie smiled up at him, loving him so fiercely she wanted to hug him close. "I'm glad somebody trusts my judgment."

"Oh, I do." Harlan eyed Logan as the younger man trotted his horse a few yards ahead of them, then slid to the ground to check a rickety fence post. "And…I also trust you to marry the right man."

Surprised, Trixie saw the expression of hope in Harlan's eyes. "You don't have to worry about Rad and me, Granddaddy. Please, don't let Mama get you all in a dither about this."

Harlan grinned. "I can handle your mother, Tricia Maria. You just take care of the rest." With that he nudged his mount into a brisk trot, throwing up his hat in a final farewell as he hurried back up the lane toward the chapel and Brant's grave.

Deciding everyone around here was acting as if they'd all taken a bad case of sun poisoning, Trixie urged her mare up to the fence where Logan struggled with the weak post. He looked so right standing there, his hat covering his curling hair, his jeans snug fitting and faded, his boots dusty and mud caked. He *was* a born cowboy, just as Brant had been. Logan belonged to this land, needed this land, to keep him strong, to keep him centered. She understood that about him, in a way Pamela had never understood about Brant.

As she watched Logan now, she knew she'd made the right decision. Pamela would be beside herself, of course. And Rad…well, she'd deal with Rad when she got back to Dallas. Right now, even though her heart was breaking, even though she knew she'd always love Logan in that special way that only first love could be cherished, she knew what she had to do. She would give him the land he held so dear, and then she'd leave him again.

When Logan looked up at last, he saw the love reflected there in her eyes, saw the struggle she'd been fighting since she'd set foot back on this place. And he decided right then and there, that no matter what she planned on doing, he had to at least offer her some comfort. He owed her that much, for Brant's memory, if nothing else.

"So you wanna talk, huh?" he said, his tone soft and yielding as he squinted up at her.

Trixie swallowed hard, gathering her strength. "Yes. I've seen enough of this place. It's time to settle things."

He walked up to her, holding her mount steady as his gaze held hers. He'd just have to go on faith, hoping that she'd made the right choice regarding her father's legacy and land. And the rest...well, he'd have to settle for what the Lord handed out. "How about I show you your daddy's sunflower patch?"

The sweetness of his suggestion washed over her with all the warmth of the morning sun, making her forget her anger and her convictions. Right now, she only wanted a truce between them, however brief.

"I'd like that," she said. Then she laughed. "Promise you won't throw me in the middle and leave me, though?"

Slinging a long, blue-jeaned leg over his saddle, he grinned then. "Oh, I might throw you down in the flower patch, but I'd never leave you."

Trixie knew he meant it. He'd always been right

here, waiting maybe, through all the years and all the doubt and pain, through his own bitterness and anger. And now she would be the one doing the leaving.

Again.

She would leave Logan to his work and his life with his son.

She would leave her heart here, too. In this land, in his hands. Always.

Chapter Seven

The legendary sunflower patch was out past one of
the far ridges, away from the hustle and bustle of the
main ranch. Logan rode the spotted pinto named
Rocky ahead of Trixie, guiding the way up to a jutting
dirt-and-rock formation. "Here we are," he said,
turning in the saddle to wait for her.

Trixie stopped her mount at the edge, then looked
out over the field of bright yellow and green giant
flowers spread out like a floral quilt below, a small
gasp of pleasure leaving her body. "Logan, it's…it's
so pretty."

Acres and acres of big, fat sunflowers lifted their
heads to follow the sun, dancing and swaying in the
warm wind. She'd never seen anything like it. And
to think, her rough-and-ready father had planted them
there. It made him all the more special in her eyes,
and filled her heart with regret.

"People come from miles around to see them,"
Logan said, pride evident in his words. "We always

have an open house during peak blooming season. For a donation, they can come and take all the pictures they want, and stay awhile to enjoy the view. People have picnics, brides have their pictures taken. Word's spread and now it's becoming a tradition.''

''What a great idea.'' She smiled over at him, thinking he had some marketing talent himself. ''I couldn't have planned a better public relations coup myself.''

He lowered his head, the hardness leaving his face as he gazed down on the flowing, rippling field. ''We just used the only draw we've got—the land. And the community is glad to give, to help the children and our mission cause.''

''And you're doing a good job. The financial reports seem in order and the records are meticulous.'' She'd looked them over last night, when she couldn't sleep. ''Of course, I did spot some places where we can improve things.''

She didn't miss the glance he shot her way. ''Nothing wrong with our record keeping, Tricia Maria.''

Giving him a level look, Trixie retorted, ''I didn't say that, Logan. I just said—oh, never mind.''

Relaxing a bit, Logan told her, ''Well, maybe we could be more efficient, but we've come a long way. Mama single-handedly learned how to run the new computer Brant had installed a few months ago. She took to the new system, after telling Brant and me she'd never get near the thing.'' He had to laugh. ''Now, she's a net surfer. Thinks we need to build our own Web site.''

Trixie laughed then, the idea of Logan's quiet, reserved mother playing around in chat rooms too paradoxical to resist. "Modern technology is frightening, but necessary. And she's right—you do need your own Web page. Especially here, where you need to be connected to some of the most remote places in the world, since you're shipping livestock and goods internationally."

He looked at her from underneath the shade of his tattered old hat, wondering if she would want to overhaul everything about the ranch—that is, if she kept the place. "Yep."

Trixie watched him, saw the doubt in his expression. "I guess you probably aren't looking forward to having me as a boss, huh?"

Logan tipped his hat back. "You know, I haven't really thought about that." Giving her a look full of promise, he added, "I can see both advantages and disadvantages in the situation. But I'd rather deal with you than some stranger who might run us all off."

And, Logan told himself, he'd just have to deal with his worries and concerns one at a time.

As the casual conversation died down, the tension mounted. Even the horses could sense it as they pranced impatiently and snorted into the humid wind.

"It's getting hot out here. Want to go down and get a closer look at the field before that sun climbs any higher?" Logan asked at last.

"Sure."

When he came around to help her down, Trixie's heart puttered and moaned, not so sure. Why did she always feel so safe, yet so scattered, in Logan's arms? Sending him a shaky smile after he set her down, she allowed him to hold her hand. "Thank you."

"Careful," he said over his shoulder. "This ridge is slippery even on a dry day."

Trixie held on, taking her time as they followed the path that led down to the open field beyond. "How do you handle all the tourists?" she asked breathlessly.

"They come in through the back way—a dirt lane that leads to the field. We just held open house a few weeks ago when the flowers were at their peak. Then Brant got sick and...we decided to cancel the second weekend."

Trixie didn't say anything. Thoughts of her father brought a great, ripping pain to her chest. She could just see him, standing here in his jeans and his cowboy hat, watching as people poured in to see the sunflowers. Such a simple thing—planting a field of flowers. Yet he'd touched so many lives by doing it. He'd brought a small measure of beauty and tranquillity to those who came here to view his creation.

She regretted that she hadn't been a part of all this, and she was once again reminded of the preacher's words about those who sow in sorrow. Had her father done that, hoping to find his joy in these beautiful, serene flowers?

By this time they'd reached the bottom of the ridge. Trixie let go of Logan's hand to rush forward and touch a flower. "They're so tall," she said as she tilted her head to view one of the massive six-foot-high blooms.

"Watch for bees," Logan warned, enjoying the way she blended in with the flowers in her yellow outfit. He didn't follow her, but chose instead to stand back and enjoy just seeing her in this field. He'd certainly pictured it enough in his mind. "He knew you loved sunflowers," he called out to her.

Trixie turned then, her eyes locking with his, her heart hammering a beat as erratic as the buzzing bees lost in the midst of the hundreds of golden petals. "He planted this for...for me?"

Logan stepped closer then, his expression full of sadness and regret. "It was his way of remembering, I guess."

She let out a long sigh. "And I always thought he'd forgotten." She couldn't bring herself to tell Logan that she'd forgotten, too. She'd forgotten that little girl who used to run wild and free amidst the bluebonnets, with her handsome father chasing her. Now she had to wonder what had happened to that child?

Logan saw the pain in her eyes and the wistful expression crossing her face. Not stopping to think, he strode toward her, then pulled her into his arms, his expression fierce with a love he'd long denied. "How could anyone forget you, Tricia Maria?"

Before she could respond, he yanked his hat off and kissed her, the heat of his mouth rivaling the heat of late September. Trixie fell into the embrace, her whole system going haywire as she allowed herself to be drawn into a wonderful dream. Too soon, however, reality pierced its way back into her consciousness, bringing with it her great shame and regret.

Pulling away, she said, "Logan, we can't do this."

His breath ragged, Logan held her with a hand on each arm, his gaze searching her face. "No, we can't, can we, because of the past, because of Rad, because I'm not good enough for you."

Seeing the hurt and anger in his eyes, she shook

her head. "Is that what you think? Is that why I never heard from you again—you think you're not good enough for me?"

He gently eased her away. "Well, I know I'm not good enough for you, and…your parents sure thought that. Your mother made that quite clear from the beginning. And yes, that was one of the reasons I never tried to find you again."

"*I* never thought that. I certainly never thought about you in that way," she admitted, tired of the lies and the deceit and all of the wasted time. "I…I loved you, Logan."

He stood there, his heart bursting with pain and love, his whole world tilting and unbalanced. Telling himself he was stepping into trouble, reminding himself he needed to be as far away from her as possible, Logan couldn't stop the need to hold her again. Just once again.

So he did, hauling her close so he could see the blue of the sky reflected in her eyes. "And I *still* love you, Tricia Maria. I will always love you."

Stunned, Trixie clung to him, her eyes going wide, her heart breaking into a million pieces. "Why didn't you come for me?" she asked, tears softening her words. "I used to lie awake at night, hoping, praying, that you'd just come to Dallas and get me and bring me back here."

"And we'd be married," he finished, a hand coming up to touch her face. "I had that same dream. I dreamed of you standing right here. I dreamed of us building a house right over there." He motioned his head, his eyes as moist as hers, then spun her around, his hands encircling her waist as he pulled her body back against his. "Your daddy gave me this ten acres, free and clear, to build a house on. But I...I never could bring myself to build anything there. I didn't have you, so what was the point?"

Trixie looked out over the valley, thinking she'd never seen a more beautiful spot. She could envision it all, her hopes, her dreams, a house with a yardful of wildflowers and sunflowers, the mountains off in the distance, cows lowing, bees humming. And...a child running to meet his father.

Her heart broke in two, because she'd given up all of her dreams the night she allowed them to take her baby away.

"Oh, Logan," she said, "we lost so much, so much."

"I know, sugar," he said, his words gentle on the back of her neck. "And...we can't get it back. It's too late now. You...you don't belong with me. You have your life mapped out, and I keep telling myself it can be a good life. I keep telling myself I can't stand in your way. I don't have the right—"

She turned then, falling back into his arms, her words ragged and torn. "No, *I* don't have the right, Logan. I don't have the right to make you miserable again. And I promised your mother—"

Logan lifted her chin, his eyes filling with alarm. "What? What did my mother tell you?"

Seeing the genuine fear and dread in his eyes, she could only shake her head. "Nothing, except she doesn't want you wasting your time on me." Then, because she was hurting so much, because she needed to know, she added, "And she told me...she told me you don't want me around your son."

He pulled her head down, his hands moving over her shoulders, then her hair. "That's not true. It's just—" He hesitated, struggled, fought against himself. "Caleb gets attached to people very easily. Sometimes he has a hard time with all the comings and goings here on the ranch, the other children passing through for a few weeks at a time. I'd hate for him to get attached to you, and then—"

Trixie finished his sentence. "And then I'll be gone out of his life for good, just like his mother."

Logan nodded, the lump in his throat almost suffocating him. "You will go, won't you? You can't bear to be here, where you committed your greatest sin with me. I remind you of your shame each time I hold you and kiss you, don't I?" The torment in his eyes increased with each question. "You're going to sell this place and never look back, right?"

She didn't have the answers to all of his questions. So she told him what was in her heart, because she couldn't tell him her real reasons for walking away. Stepping back, she lifted her gaze and stared up at him. "I'm not going to sell the ranch, Logan. In fact, I'm going to do just the opposite."

At the look of hope on his face, she held up a hand. "I want to put you in charge completely. I'll trust you to do all the things my father set out to do, but—"

"But you don't want to be involved." This time he finished her statement, his expression torn between relief and regret.

"I can't be involved," she stressed, her hand on his arm. "There's just too many memories, Logan. Too much water under the bridge for us—and too much temptation between us right now. I'd only be in the way here, and I don't want you to wind up resenting me.''

''So I'm still not good enough for you.''

Wrapping her arms around her waist, she shook her head again. She wanted to tell him that she wasn't good enough for him, after the horrible thing she'd done. ''I didn't say that. I told you, I've never felt that way.''

''But you never bothered to come back to me. And now, you're planning on leaving me again. Does it matter that I still love you?''

She heard the doubt in his voice, saw the hard edges of his bitter smile. ''More than you'll ever know,'' she said as she started back up the ridge, afraid she'd crumble and confess if she didn't get a grip on herself.

He caught up with her, urging her around with a firm tug. ''Then stay. Stay here with me, Trixie.''

In that one moment Trixie saw everything with a brilliant clarity. She did belong here, and she did love Logan. She'd never stopped loving him. But he could never know that. Because if he knew what she'd done, he'd never forgive her. Her secret, her choice, would destroy him.

And so she didn't tell him what was really in her heart.

When she didn't respond, Logan let her go, dropping his hands to his side in defeat. Then he looked off into the distance, to the empty patch of land her father had deeded to him. ''Guess I'll never get that house built. I don't want to live in it alone.''

When he pushed past her, she tried to stop him.

Maybe she should just go ahead and tell him the truth. It would certainly change his opinion of her and stop him from pining away, as Gayle had feared. "Logan?"

But Logan was beyond listening now. She'd made her choice, and once again he wasn't included in her plans. Really, he should be glad, relieved, that she wouldn't be hovering around here. He didn't need her here, and he sure didn't want her here. He only wanted to protect his son. "I'm grateful that you aren't selling, Trixie," he said from his perch on the rocks. "And I won't let you down. I'll take care of things here. I'm not going anywhere."

"Thank you," she said, the coward in her relieved that she hadn't had to open up and reveal her great secret to him. "I appreciate that."

He reached out a hand to help her climb back up to the horses. When they reached the top, Trixie looked back out over the field of sunflowers and wished she didn't have to go back to Dallas. But what choice did she have? She still loved Rad, but she would *always* love Logan. This situation really wasn't fair to either of them.

Logan waited as she mounted her horse, then he turned to her, his gaze focused and blank. "This is for the best. Like I said, you don't belong here."

With that he trotted the pinto ahead of her, leaving her alone on the ridge while a great, sighing wind rushed through the yellow field of flowers down below. Trixie listened to that hot, moaning wind, then sent up a prayer for help. Had she made the right choice?

"You're wrong, Logan," she whispered. "I do belong here, but I can't stay. I can't."

Unless she told everyone the truth at last, including Rad. What if she simply confessed her great sin to everyone and let God handle the rest? It would be risky; she could wind up losing both Rad and Logan. But at least she'd be free, free and clear, to have a future with hope, a future with no shame and no secrets. And maybe a little forgiveness.

She turned her prancing horse and stared out over the elegant sunflowers, her mind at peace for the first time since her father's death. "Thanks, Daddy," she said.

She knew what she had to do now.

"What should we do?" Samantha asked Logan later that afternoon as they tried to round up a flock of about fifty sheep that had burst through the weak place in the fence Logan had spotted earlier that morning.

"I'll saddle a horse," Logan said, watching as the timid sheep spilled out into the lane and headed for the back forty. "You and one of the older kids can take the four-wheeler."

"Can I ride the four-wheeler, Daddy?" Caleb asked, always his father's shadow when Logan was anywhere near the main house.

Logan bent to scoop his son up in his arms. "Nope, you know the rules. You aren't old enough yet to ride the four-wheeler with anyone but me, son." Seeing the disappoint in his son's eyes, he added, "How 'bout you ride shotgun with me on Rocky?"

Caleb's eyes lit up. "Let me get my hat."

In spite of sheep milling around where they weren't supposed to be, Logan grinned. Caleb was a little cowboy himself, following a long tradition. And chomping at the bit to follow the bigger kids around the ranch on their various chores. Gayle had to watch the kid every minute, or he'd try to sneak by her and go off to the far reaches of the ranch. Since his grandmother was overprotective by nature, Caleb rarely got a chance to get into any heavy mischief. But when he did, it made up for the rest.

"How'd this happen, anyway?" Logan asked Samantha, speaking of mischief. He had a sneaking feeling one of his young charges probably provoked the sheep to stampede.

Samantha threw her long cornrows off her shoulder and gave him a beseeching look. "Promise you won't scream?"

"Just tell me the truth," Logan said, holding on to the last shreds of his patience. If he hadn't been so distracted with Trixie, so busy confessing his undying love to her, he would have fixed this when he'd first spotted it. Glad this had happened in spite of the mess, he reckoned he'd needed a wake-up call. This ranch was his first priority. He'd better remember that.

"It was during the worming," Samantha began. "We had four adult volunteers helping, including Mr. Harlan, but you know how that goes. Mr. Harlan knew what to do, but the rest—"

"Yeah." Logan nodded. Volunteers were sometimes more of a pain than a help. "Somebody get skittish or something?"

"One of the ladies saw a big spider out behind the worming station," Samantha tried to explain.

"And she screamed bloody murder?"

"No, actually, she was pretty calm. Her husband did all the hopping up and down and screaming. Just enough to cause the sheep to get jittery and run for the nearest fence."

Logan sighed as he headed to the stables in a backward trot. "I get the picture. Hurry, now, and bring the four-wheeler. And keep those volunteers away from the herd."

"Right." Samantha turned to head to the open garage behind the barn, afraid to tell Logan that Mr. Harlan had already taken the volunteers down the lane on foot to waylay the anxious sheep. Spotting Trixie coming toward her, she waved. "Gotta go, Miss Trixie. Sheep on the loose."

"I wondered what all the fuss was about," Trixie said, her gaze on the renegade animals heading gleefully to freedom. All afternoon she'd been cloistered in the tiny office in one corner of the lodge, going over the computer printouts and farm reports with Harlan, in order to keep her mind off Logan. After giving her his blessings and telling her he was fully behind her decision to keep the ranch, Harlan, always the rancher himself, had come out earlier to help with the chores.

Now, Trixie had stepped out for some fresh air and exercise only to find chaos. "Want some help?"

Samantha looked skeptical. Since Logan seemed to tense up every time Blondie was around, she wasn't too sure about accepting Trixie's well-intended services. "Logan told me to keep all the amateurs away."

"I've been on cattle drives," Trixie replied, affronted. "I think I can manage a few sheep."

"Well, come on, then. I gotta hurry."

Trixie followed her to the shed to get the four-wheeler, thinking sheep herding was a little different from cattle herding. Her Daddy had always relied on a horse. Spying Logan and Caleb already following the sheep astride Rocky, she smiled in spite of her earlier morose mood. Caleb was enjoying being with his daddy up on the spotted beauty. And his hat was about as ratty and stained as Logan's. The two looked so beautiful, so perfect riding atop the great horse, that her heart again felt heavy with regret. That little boy needed a mother.

And she...she suddenly realized she needed a child.

Maybe she could convince Rad to reconsider his stance on waiting, so they could have children soon. Maybe that would replace this great emptiness in her heart.

"Hang on," Samantha warned as they headed after the sheep, the four-wheeler whirling and circling back to change the flock's erratic course.

Snapping to attention, Trixie did as she was told, since her body bounced and hopped with the terrain. Soon, however, Samantha and Logan and the few other daring souls under Harlan's experienced hand, had the reluctant runaways corralled back in the broken paddock.

Caleb stood proudly with his daddy, holding the fence together with the help of some of the other workers, while Logan temporarily patched the damaged spot back together.

Watching them, Trixie remembered Logan's earlier words, wishing it were as easy to fix broken relationships. "I still love you." She'd tried so hard to block those words out of her system this afternoon, through tedious reports, through phone calls back to her own office, through thoughts of her upcoming wedding. But Logan's words and his kisses haunted her and held her. Even Harlan had wondered if something else was bothering her. Her grandfather was shrewd; he would figure things out soon enough if she wasn't careful.

She needed to go home. After all, there was really nothing holding her here now that she'd made her decision. Except the memory of Logan's kiss and the fact that he still loved her. How long would that love last, though, if he knew the truth?

As the dust settled, Trixie came off the four-wheeler with a wave, unsure about Logan's reaction to her help since they'd parted on such uncertain ground this morning.

. But instead of frowning at her, he started laughing. "You look like you've been rode hard and put up wet," he chided as he reached out to wipe a smudge of dirt off her face.

Realizing she was covered in dust and grit and that her hair had been completely rearranged from the wind and humidity, Trixie had to smile. "Guess I look pretty stupid, all decked out in sunflowers and covered with mud. Kind of wilted and dusty, huh?"

Logan's eyes burned softly, while his tone became intimate. "You look all right to me, but the dust…well, that's another thing all together. I think you better let Mama wash that outfit for you.''

Seeing the mud spots and various other stains splattered across her intricately woven sunflowers, Trixie shook her head and wrinkled her nose. ''It has to be hand washed. I'll do it myself.''

Caleb tugged on her grimy shorts. ''Miss Trixie, wanna see those kittens now?''

Trixie looked over to Logan for approval. When she saw the grudging admiration in his eyes, along with some other unreadable emotion, she hesitated. ''I don't think—''

''It's all right,'' Logan said, dusting off his forever dusty hat before he plopped it back on his dark curls. ''In fact, I'd like to see those kittens myself. Mind if I tag along?''

Caleb reached out a hand to both his father and his new friend, tugging the two of them along as he walked between. ''We don't mind, do we, Miss Trixie?''

Trixie's gaze met Logan's over the boy's head. ''Not at all.''

In spite of the brittle smile on his face, she once again sensed a hesitancy in Logan. Was he coming with them to make sure she didn't do or say anything to upset his son? Or was he worried about something else entirely?

Trixie didn't have time to ponder that puzzle. From up the lane toward the lodge, someone called her name.

''Tricia?''

Her heart did a quick jolt. Only one person ever called her by her first name, without the Maria. Still holding Caleb's hand, she turned to find Radford Randolph heading toward her, his silk suit coat tucked over one arm, his face covered with sweat and irritation.

"Rad?" She whispered the name, a panic setting in to make her blood run faster and her heart pump harder. Her gaze flew to Logan's. She didn't miss the condemnation in his eyes as he lifted one brow in a daring question.

"Who's that dude?" Caleb asked with the innocence of a seven-year-old.

"That *dude* is no one for us to worry about," Logan said, tight-lipped. "Show me those kittens, son."

Caleb held back, his big eyes lifting to his father. "But what about Miss Trixie?"

Logan shot her another scathing look. "Miss Trixie has unexpected company. Let's leave her alone so she can have some privacy with her intended."

Torn, Trixie felt Caleb's little hand slip away from her own. She stood frozen in place, her eyes on Rad, her heart heavy with guilt as Logan's words replayed over and over in her mind. "I still love you."

But she'd promised her love to Rad. And now he was here. Watching helplessly as Caleb and Logan headed toward the stables without her, Trixie decided she'd had enough of the deceit. After all, she couldn't possibly expect to start a new life with Rad without telling him the truth.

It was only fair. And he loved her. He'd forgive her. He had to.

Because she couldn't stay here.

As Logan had pointed out so bitterly, she didn't belong here. She belonged with Rad. She'd just have to take her chances and hope she was doing the right thing for both of the men she loved.

Or, she told herself with a wry smile, maybe she was doing this because she was afraid of happiness.

She certainly didn't believe she deserved any.

Chapter Eight

"Hello, darling," Rad said, reaching out to give Trixie a hug. The look of her ruined outfit stopped him, though. Instead, he leaned toward her in an awkward position, staring at her as if he'd never seen her before. "Good grief, what happened to you?"

"Sheep stampede," she said, still in shock and wishing she could just drop through the earth. "It's a long story."

Rad nodded, then shot her an unsure smile. "Well, you'll be fine once you get cleaned up. Right?"

Annoyed that he didn't even want to kiss her hello, Trixie started walking toward the lodge. Rad was a germ freak, afraid to leave his apartment at the slightest hint of anything odd in the Metroplex air. "Don't worry, Rad, it's not contagious."

He hurried after her, his chuckle as brittle as his thick, sandy blond hair. "Of course it isn't. And I'm sorry if I seem a little...surprised. It's just that I've never seen you this way."

Trixie turned to face him, glad to see him in spite of her ill temper. She couldn't blame him; she'd never allowed him to see her at anything but her best. Another of Pamela's rules—never leave home without your makeup or your hair perfectly in place. "It's all right. I guess I do look like a fright. What on earth are you doing here, anyway?"

He shifted his feet, stepping gingerly so his Italian loafers didn't sink into anything mushy or smelly. "I was worried about you. You've been here a few days now, and you haven't returned any of my calls. "Pamela—"

Trixie groaned, so frustrated with her mother's misguided interference, she didn't bother telling him she'd tried to return his calls but kept missing him. "Don't tell me she sent you to check up on me, too. Granddaddy's already here."

"Harlan's here?"

Hearing the worry in his question, Trixie had to smile. Rad had always been intimidated by her grandfather. And she knew Harlan reveled in that intimidation, just to keep her fiancé on his toes. Funny, Logan seemed to get along quite nicely with Harlan. But then, very little intimidated Logan.

Mentally shaking away the comparison, Trixie continued. "Yes, he's here. He's in the paddock, trying to worm sheep."

A look of distaste twisted Rad's handsome, clean-cut face. Carefully touching a hand to her arm, he said, "Why are you doing this, Tricia?"

"Doing what?"

"Hanging around this rundown old ranch. I thought we agreed to sell it right away."

Tired, dirty, smelly and completely out of whack, Trixie glared up at him. "*We* didn't agree to anything, Radford. You wanted me to sell, but I told you I wanted to think about it. And…I have."

He smiled, then, oblivious to her frustrations. "Good. Then my timing is perfect. We can fly home together."

Not in a mood to be manipulated, Trixie dug her heels in. "I'm not ready to go home."

"And why not? If you've arranged for a buyer—"

Bracing herself for what was about to come, she said, "I'm not selling."

Rad's face went from pasty to pink. "What did you say?"

"I said, I'm not selling this ranch. I've done enough research to get a handle on things around here, and I like what I see. My father was providing a much-needed service to a lot of less fortunate people, and I intend to see that his work here continues."

Swatting a fly away impatiently, Rad placed a hand on his hip. "You can't be serious? You know you don't have time for all this do-gooder stuff. What about your position back in Dallas? You worked very hard to become head of marketing, and well, something like this could ruin all of that."

Anger coloring her words, she asked, "Are you referring to my position as a marketing consultant, or my position in polite society?"

"Well, both. I mean, think of all the time you'll be forced to invest in this—this money pit. If you want to donate to your father's favorite charity, sell this place and set up a trust or something, so we can write it off."

Leave it to Rad to find some way to justify being generous! "I don't want to do that," she said, her tone firm. "I've made my decision, and I've put Logan in charge. My father's mission work will go on as planned, and I intend to be involved in it as much as possible."

Rad looked at her as if she had the plague. "When did you get so high-and-mighty?" he asked with a snort.

Keeping her hurt feelings to herself, Trixie said, "When I realized that my father was a better Christian than I'll ever be."

Lifting a finger to point in her face, Rad gave her a look of indignation. "You could have at least discussed this with me, Tricia. You know how I feel about being saddled with this place."

"It's my place, Rad," she reminded him kindly, though she felt anything but, "and it was my decision." Giving him a disappointed look, she added, "And I knew you'd try to talk me out of it. But it's final. I'm going to tie up a few loose ends, consult with the local lawyers Daddy hired, then I'll be home by the end of the week."

He stepped closer, his nose turning up at the smell of animal all around them. "Does this have something to do with that Logan fellow?"

Shocked, Trixie immediately became wary. "What makes you think that?"

Rad studied her face, his own expression disapproving. "Pamela told me you once had a crush on him. Of course, she said she nipped it in the bud right away."

Furious at her mother's deliberate betrayal, Trixie

wanted to tell him the truth right then and there. But when she spotted Logan and Caleb walking toward them from the stables, she held herself in check, knowing that would be a fatal mistake.

Instead, she simply said, "My mother would say anything to discredit Logan. She's never liked the ranch or any of the people who work here. But then she's never bothered to come up here and see exactly what I've seen."

Rad rolled his eyes heavenward. "Well, I'm here and I'm not overly impressed. And I'd really like to know what's going on. Just what have you seen, Tricia?"

Trixie stepped closer then, hoping to keep her words low pitched, so Logan wouldn't hear her. "I don't like the implication of your question, Rad."

"Why? Do you have something to hide?"

What would he do when she told him the truth? Right this minute she didn't care. He was being so callous, so condemning, she didn't like him at all. And he had once again sided with her mother. That hurt the worst.

Before she could respond, Rad pushed her away. "That smell is going to cause me to start sneezing. Please, go and change, so we can talk like two sensible adults."

That's when Logan stalked across the yard, his eyes blazing fire, his temper boiling. "Hey, Ralph, the lady's had a hard day. Cut her some slack."

Rad glared over at Logan with complete disgust. "The name's Radford. Radford Randolph. And who are you?"

Logan's tone was mocking. "Logan. Logan Maxwell—the one she *used* to have the crush on."

Trixie realized their voices had carried out over the trees and that Logan had heard enough to get him riled. Afraid he'd say more than she wanted him to say, she placed a hand on his chest. "I can handle this, Logan. Thank you."

"Can you?" he asked, the accusation in his question only rubbing her already-raw pride.

"Yes, I can," she said between a clenched jaw. She was getting a splitting headache, and she needed a long, hot shower. "Rad's right. I need to clean up. He can cool his engines in the cookhouse while I change."

Looking over at Rad, she suggested on a more level tone, "Why don't you spend the night, and in the morning I'll show you around." Maybe if she showed him the work being done here, she could make him see why she wanted to keep this place.

Logan interjected, "You're welcome to bunk in the camp house. It's not too crowded right now. Only 'bout a half a dozen teenagers."

Rad lifted a hand in dismissal, his gold Rolex glinting in the waning late afternoon sun. "Forget that. I doubt either Trixie or I will be staying past supper."

Trixie whirled to face him, her voice impatient. "I told you, I'm not ready to come home yet."

Rad looked from her to Logan. "And whose idea was that?"

Logan held out his hands, palms up. "Hey, fellow, Trixie makes her own decisions. Or hadn't you even noticed?"

"Stop it," Trixie said, stepping between them as

they both pawed the ground like two raging bulls about to butt heads. "Logan, your son is watching from the porch."

That got Logan's attention, forcing him to shut down his overactive temper. "Yeah, thanks for reminding me."

Trixie sensed a hidden meaning in his words, but she let it go. With Rad here, she had more than enough to worry about. And it would get much worse once she told him everything.

"It wasn't right of your ma to send him up here," Harlan said later as he huddled close to his granddaughter in the cookhouse. All around them, teenagers sat laughing and talking to the few remaining volunteers, their mouths full of Gayle's famous spaghetti and garlic bread, their eyes full of hope and contentment. This was the Wednesday-night ranch supper, a celebration for both the students and the volunteers who'd helped that day, so everyone was included, and expected, to be here.

Trixie had readily agreed to help out, and she'd actually looked forward to her meal with the youth and the volunteers, that is, until Rad had shown up. Now she was torn between giving her attention to the camp kids and her cranky fiancé.

Watching him now, she whispered to Harlan, "I'd better get back to him. He's waiting on his glass of iced tea."

"He can get his own drink," Harlan replied, frowning.

Trixie ignored him and went to sit back down beside Rad. "Did you enjoy the spaghetti?"

Rad pushed the remains of his meal away. "The sauce is a little too sweet for my taste."

Wanting to make amends, Trixie said, "How about dessert? Gayle makes wonderful chocolate chip cookies."

Giving her a look of disdain, Rad retorted, "I don't want a cookie. I'm not some waif off the street, you know. I just want you to come back to Dallas with me."

Needing some answers, Trixie asked, "Did you come up here because you missed me, or because my mother talked you into coming?"

He glanced down at his plate. "Well, I do have a pretty heavy caseload. That's why I have to get back, tonight if possible."

"You didn't answer my question."

He took her hand then. "You should already know the answer. Yes, I missed you, but Pamela did suggest—"

Trixie pulled her hand away. "Just as I thought."

Offended, Rad said, "Hey, don't get mad at your mother. She's worried sick about you, and after seeing the looks of some of these delinquents, I can understand why."

"They are not delinquents," Trixie said, keeping her voice low. "These are children, Rad. Children who needed some guidance and some love to set them on the right path. They're not bad kids—they've just had some bad breaks."

"If you say so."

Getting up, she gave him a sad smile. "I know so. The people who work here have done wonders with the children who pass through this ranch. That's one of the reasons I don't want to change anything.''

"You've obviously been impulsive," Rad told her. "You've let some sort of sentimentality cloud your better judgment."

Hurt and aggravated by his attitude, Trixie said, "Yes, I guess I have. But I'm not going to sell this ranch. And that's final."

Her heart swelled with pride, knowing that her father had saved so many young people from a life of crime and abandonment. She'd seen the pictures of past Camp Dunaway participants, and she'd read the letters students had sent to her father, thanking him for taking the time to help them out. Somehow she knew in her heart God was giving her an opportunity to make a difference, and to find the right priorities in her own life. She couldn't just walk away from a challenge and responsibility of that magnitude. She'd just have to make Rad see things her way.

"Can't you understand how important this is?" she asked him.

"No," he said, a pout distorting his face.

Losing her patience, Trixie said, "I'm going to talk to Granddaddy."

"What about us? What about leaving?"

"I'm not leaving tonight, Rad," she repeated, gritting her teeth with each word.

Coming back to Harlan, who'd witnessed the whole exchange with an eagle eye, she said, "I can't really blame Rad. He's just concerned about me. And you know how mother is. When she wants things to go her way, she pulls out the stops. Especially when it comes to interfering in my life. So I'm not surprised she talked him into coming up here. I am surprised, though, that she didn't book you two on a flight together, or better yet, fuel up the company jet.''

Harlan snorted, then lowered his head, looking guilty. ''Well, actually, she had planned it that way. Only I jumped the gun and took off without him. I didn't think he'd have the gumption to come on his own, though.''

Amazed at her grandfather's devious ways, Trixie could only stare at him, thinking perhaps Brant had inherited his good-ol'-boy charm naturally. ''Thanks for trying, Granddaddy,'' she said. ''You'll be in trouble when you get back home. We both will.''

''We'll cross that bridge when we come to it,'' Harlan replied sagely. ''*Are* you going back with him?'' he asked, his voice low and gruff as he eyed Rad, who sat sulking in a corner.

Rad had not been happy when Trixie informed him they had to share dinner with the entire group. He'd wanted a more intimate meal. And to top things off, Logan was conspicuously absent, which meant he was probably off somewhere stewing.

Her headache pounded against her temple with each pulse beat. ''No, I'm not,'' she replied to Harlan's question. ''That's why he's over there pouting. I plainly told him I can't leave until the end of the week—probably Sunday.''

Harlan winked over at her. ''A lot can happen before Sunday, sweetheart.''

''A lot has happened already,'' she admitted, knowing she could trust her grandfather. ''I've discovered so much about my father, and myself for that matter, that I didn't know. And I'm so proud of him.

I want to do the right thing. And I believe keeping the ranch is right. It's what he would have wanted me to do. But it will be a tremendous responsibility. I...I just need to sort through it all, I guess.''

Harlan nodded. ''This place has a way of doing that to a person. Really makes you think about what matters most in this old life.'' He patted her arm affectionately. ''And I, young lady, am very proud of you. Always have been. If you're worried about the burden of running this place, you know you can count on me. I only wish your father had turned to me more.''

''Me, too,'' she said, her thoughts misting over with regret. ''He did all of this on his own, maybe because he was so hurt by Mother's rejection, maybe because he needed to carve out his own special niche in the world. He was a good man—I know that. I think I always knew it. But I sure wish he'd...he'd stayed closer to all of us.''

''Too late for worrying about that,'' Harlan replied, his words gruff with emotion. ''My son was full of conflict and contradictions—a cowboy who had a hard time with rules and regulations, which is why your mama could never tame him.''

Without thinking, Trixie said, ''Logan's a lot like that.''

Harlan gave her a scrutinizing look, then nodded. ''Yep. A good man, proud and stubborn, and willing to work hard to keep this place intact. You're smart to put him in charge of things. He won't let you down.''

Surprised by her grandfather's impassioned praise,

Trixie glanced toward him. "Why, Granddaddy, I had no idea you admired Logan Maxwell so much."

Harlan's aged eyes grew intense with meaning. "Like I told you, I want you to marry the right man."

Confused, Trixie shot him a questioning look. "If I didn't know better, I'd think you're suggesting I marry Logan instead of Rad."

He shrugged. "I didn't say that."

"Uh-huh. And what you don't say always tells me more than what you do say." Pausing, she glanced around, then whispered, "How do you really feel...about Logan?"

Harlan chuckled low. "I've got a better question. How do *you* feel about Logan?"

"Granddaddy, you sly old thing," she admonished, glad that he'd always been honest with her, even if he could read her like a book. Then, turning serious, she said, "I still care about him. I guess I always will. But we both agree that it's for the best if we just go our separate ways."

"You sure about that?"

Watching Rad, she had to wonder. "Right now, I'm not sure about anything."

"Better be sure before you make a mistake you can't fix," Harlan warned her. "Constant prayer and careful consideration, that's my advice. Now, I'm going back for seconds on that spaghetti."

Trixie sat still, thinking her grandfather's words echoed the same warning Logan had given her. If she were honest with herself, she'd admit she wanted to tell Rad the truth to test him, to see if he would stand by her. She had the sinking feeling he wouldn't. It made her realize that all the money and position in the world couldn't bring her what she really wanted.

She wanted someone to care enough about her to fight for her, really fight for her, in spite of her shortcomings. She'd always tried to be the perfect daughter, putting on a proper face for society, putting up with her mother's requests and reprimands, yet always believing she was loved and cherished. But when she'd failed, when she'd digressed, Pamela had hidden her away in shame...too afraid of a scandal to stand by her daughter or show any compassion for Trixie's feelings. And even her father and Harlan had gone along with it, to keep things quiet, to protect the Dunaway name. Would Rad stand by her because he truly loved her? Or would he too turn away in shame and disgust?

Wanting to rekindle the good she'd seen in him when Pamela had first introduced them all those months ago, she got up to go sit by him again. "I'm sorry," she said in an attempt to console him. "I know all of this had been hard on you, and I really want to make you understand why I'm doing this. Do you want to go for a walk and talk?"

Rad pushed his fork through his half-eaten spaghetti. "Is there anyplace around here that doesn't smell like a cow pasture?"

"Not really," she said, laughing. "We could go back to the lodge and sit on the screened porch. It's downwind from the paddocks, and the flies can't get to us there."

"Okay." His eyes still on her, he rose from his seat, then turned to grab his coat. His hand moved over the silk, then stopped. "Trixie, my watch is gone."

Alarmed, she looked around. "What? Are you sure?"

"Yes, I'm sure," he said impatiently. "I took it off when we all had to freshen up camp style earlier. I put it in my coat pocket."

"Maybe it fell out of your coat."

Rad immediately panicked. "No, I'm telling you it's gone." He glared at the suddenly quiet teenagers who'd been watching him shyly all evening. "Who took my watch?"

Hearing him, Gayle walked around from the kitchen area, her expression full of contempt. "What's the problem?"

Rad shouted at her. "I'll tell you the problem. Somebody took my watch from the pocket of my coat." His gaze accused each and everyone of them.

Trixie hissed at him. "Rad, don't be silly. Let's look for it."

"I don't need to look," he said, anger blotching his face. "Somebody had better start talking, or I'm calling the sheriff. That was a very expensive watch."

Wondering where Logan was, Trixie tried to hush Rad again. "Please, don't jump to conclusions. Where did you last have the watch?"

"Near that big basin outside where everybody washed their hands," he replied hotly. "If I'd been allowed to go to the lodge, this wouldn't have happened. I took it off because I didn't want it to accidentally go down that big, dirty drain."

Thinking the watch was waterproof and built to stay put, Trixie remembered Logan had deliberately insisted Rad stand in the wash line to the outdoor sink so all the adults could set an example to the young people—no one got special privileges here. His way of getting the upper hand, she supposed. And just to show him what an inconvenience it had been, Rad had purposely taken his watch off and rolled up the sleeves of his white shirt. But surely none of the children had stolen Rad's precious piece of jewelry.

"Then let's look outside by the washing basin," she suggested, her tone soothing and sure.

Rad stomped away while Trixie explained to the puzzled teenagers what had happened. Samantha started an immediate search, a worried expression on her face. Harlan, skeptical and keen eyed, joined in with the rest of the volunteers. Gayle huffed, then went back into the kitchen to clean up.

But where was Logan?

Racing around the cookhouse, Trixie searched the grounds for him. It wasn't like him to be late for supper with the kids, especially a celebration supper where he expected everyone to be on equal footing and their best behavior.

Then she saw him there in the red rays of the sunset, and her heart stopped. He'd had a shower and now wore a clean set of faded jeans and a fresh T-shirt, his hair still wet with dark, damp curls springing up around his temples. He stood oblivious to the commotion off in the distance, because he was intensely busy with his own secretive work. He was hanging her sunflower shorts out on the clothesline behind the lodge.

The outfit was obviously damp and…completely

clean. Not a bit of mud remained on the bright garments. They looked brand-new.

"Logan?" she called as she hurried toward him. "What on earth—"

He turned then, guilty and sheepish, his eyes rich with a sweetness that took her breath away. "You said hand wash."

Trixie stopped, her gaze moving over his face. "You washed my outfit?"

He didn't answer. Instead he gave her an indifferent shrug, then turned around to finish pinning the clothes to the line.

"That's the sweetest thing anyone's ever done for me," she said, her heart opening like a flower bud finding the sun.

"Don't go around talking about it," he replied drily. "I've got a reputation to maintain."

She smiled as he turned to face her. "I won't tell."

For a long time they just stood there, looking at each other, the brilliant rays of the evening sun falling all around them in golden shards, neither one of them able to say what was really on their minds.

And there in that knowing light Trixie discovered what her soul had been shouting at her from the first time she'd seen him again—she loved him with all her heart. And she wanted to tell him. Not only that, but she wanted, needed, to tell him the whole truth, and hope, pray, for his forgiveness. Her grandfather had said Logan wouldn't let her down. She'd find out, one way or another.

"Logan—"

"Why, you little punk!"

Rad's angry shout brought her head around, forcing her to forget about telling Logan anything for now.

"What's going on?" Logan asked, pushing past her to head to the cookhouse where Rad stood with a cluster of teenagers. Soon Harlan and Gayle and the others had joined them.

Trixie followed Logan, meaning to stop him from provoking another fight with Rad, or worse. She hoped Rad hadn't been right. She didn't believe anyone had taken his watch, but it might have proved too tempting for someone who'd never seen such an exquisite piece of jewelry before.

She prayed none of the children had given in to that temptation. And she prayed neither Logan or Rad would do anything foolish or rash if they had.

Chapter Nine

Horrified, Trixie watched as Rad yanked little Caleb by the arm, his face distorted with anger, his whole body rigid with accusation.

"You took my watch, didn't you?"

Before Rad could question the boy further, Logan pushed between them, the force of his hand on Rad's arm causing Rad to glance up.

"Let him go. Now," Logan said on a steely calm breath.

Rad pushed Logan's arm away in irritation, but realizing everybody was watching him manhandle a child, he reluctantly let Caleb go. The frightened child burst into tears, then ran to his grandmother's arms.

Logan glared at Rad, then turned to the little boy. "Caleb, did you take Mr. Randolph's watch?"

Caleb gulped back a sob, then stared wide-eyed up at his father before handing the missing watch over to Logan. Trixie could see the fear in the boy's eyes.

Even if Caleb had stolen the watch, Rad had no right to be so cruel to a child....

Logan squatted down in front of his son, then touched a gentle arm to Caleb's shoulder. "Just tell the truth, son. I promise you aren't in trouble unless you did something wrong."

A look of trust slowly emerged through the tears Caleb couldn't hide. "I...I found it, Daddy," he said, his words filled with a plea. He pointed to the wall of the cookhouse. "Over there by the flower bed."

Logan looked around the group, his voice calm in spite of his racing heart. "Did anybody else see anything?"

Marco stepped forward, shifting his weight from foot to foot. "He's telling the truth, Mr. Logan. When Mr. Randolph told us his watch was missing, we all came out to look...and Caleb found it over in those yellow mums by the washbasin."

Rad hissed, then placed both hands on his hips. "You don't actually believe that, do you?" Pointing an accusing finger at the two young boys, he said, "I saw those two huddled together, snickering. I'm telling you—they took it."

Marco shook his head. "No, sir, we were happy because we were so glad we'd found it. Caleb couldn't wait to show it to you."

Caleb, embarrassed now, hid his head against his grandmother's apron.

Trixie's heart went out to him. She knew from being around him, and hearing his grandmother talk, that Caleb was inclined to be impish at times, but she didn't think he had deliberately taken Rad's watch.

Rad still looked skeptical though. "I'm sorry, I just

don't believe that. You both looked guilty when I caught you with it.''

''That's because you seemed so mad when you shouted at us,'' Marco said, his voice low and shaky. ''You scared us.''

Logan stood up, his nose inches from Rad's, his level tone belying the heated look in his eyes. ''If they say they didn't do it, then I believe them.'' Touching Caleb on the shoulder, he added, ''My son's been taught to tell the truth, and Marco knows the rules regarding other people's property.''

Rad looked surprised to learn the little boy was Logan's son, but the knowledge didn't stop his ranting; it only added fuel to his self-righteous fire. ''Well, you know how kids can be, especially if they're allowed to run around *unsupervised.*'' His condescending tone and the way his eyes glinted when they centered on Logan indicated that he didn't think highly of Logan's parenting skills, or this whole setup. ''We all know why most of these children wound up here, anyway. Maybe your son's learned a thing or two from some of them. I think he's just afraid to admit he took it.''

Shocked and embarrassed, Trixie stepped forward to touch his arm. ''Rad, Caleb wouldn't do such a thing. Besides, he was being supervised, as are *all* of the children entrusted here. Caleb was in the cookhouse kitchen with Gayle most of the evening, so he never had an opportunity to go through your pockets.''

''I was sitting right by the kitchen door,'' Rad shot back, his tone defensive. ''It would have been easy for him to sneak around and take it.'' Scowling at her, he added, "Why are you defending these people, anyway?"

Trixie looked from the man she had pledged to marry, down to the confused little boy in baggy denim shorts and a baseball shirt, still clinging to his grand-mother's skirts. Her eyes soft and gentle on Caleb, she said, "Because I believe Caleb when he says he found the watch. Everyone saw you take it off right in that very spot, Rad. Be reasonable. The watch slipped out of your coat pocket, and I for one, think you owe Caleb and Marco an apology."

Rad snorted, then threw his hands up in the air. "Fine, fine, have it your way." Leaning forward, he said in an exaggerated voice, "I'm so sorry. Now, could I just have my watch back."

Logan shoved the glinting gold at him, a look of contempt etching his face. "The excitement's over, folks," he said to the awkward, embarrassed crowd. Giving Rad a meaningful look, he added, "Let's all be more careful with our valuables from now on."

Rad started to retort, but at the warning look from Harlan, decided better of it.

As the crowd dispersed, Trixie headed over to Caleb. "Are you okay, sweetie?"

Gayle, for once, didn't pull the child away. Instead she nudged Caleb forward. "Tell Miss Trixie thanks for sticking by you, Caleb."

"Thank you," the little boy said, his eyes still bright with tears. "I did find it over there, Miss Trixie. My Daddy taught me not to steal, and besides I got a Cal Ripken, Jr., watch for my birthday, any-way. Mr. Brant gave it to me. I don't need another one."

Placing both hands on the boy's shoulders, Trixie smiled. "Cal Ripken, huh? Well, he's a baseball legend. You're right. Your watch is much more valuable than that plain old gold one.'''

Distracted from his woes, Caleb perked up considerably. "You like baseball?"

"Astros and Rangers," she answered, glad she'd taken his mind off this humiliating situation. "Jeff Bagwell is my favorite Astros player. Maybe they'll make it to the play-offs, huh?"

"Sure hope so. My friend Matt, he loves Jeff Bagwell. He's got all of his cards." With that, the little boy ran off into the sunset, his tears forgotten.

But his father hadn't forgotten. Logan watched as the last of the young people and volunteers sauntered off to the bunkhouse to watch a video, then turned back to Rad.

Getting in the man's face so Rad could see the mad in his eyeballs, Logan said, "If you ever lay a hand on my son again, I'll personally see to it that you lose more than your Rolex."

Rad looked unsure, then scoffed, quickly recovering. "You're in no position to be ordering me around, Maxwell. Pretty soon, I'll be co-owner of this ranch. I suggest you keep that in mind before you make any idle threats."

Gritting his teeth to keep from belting the man, Logan used every bit of confrontational counseling he'd been taught over the years, as well as a deep reserve of inner strength. While it galled him to let this idiot get away with a slur like that, he knew he had to maintain his cool for his son's sake and for the benefit of the other kids here.

His eyes on Trixie, he said, "Don't remind me."
Then he turned back to Rad, his stance unyielding.
"You might eventually own this ranch through marriage to Trixie, but neither one of you will ever own
me. Just stay away from my son."

But Rad didn't know when to quit. "Hey, Maxwell, I've got a better idea. Why don't you and your
brat pack up and get off this property! Sure would
save all of us the trouble later."

Logan's hand on Rad's throat was a blur of motion.
Trixie watched as he shoved Rad up against the wall
of the cookhouse, rattling the screen door in the pro-
cess.

Gayle's shocked gasp echoed out over the night,
causing Trixie to bolt into action.

Rushing forward, with Harlan on the other side, she
managed to pull Logan off Rad. "Stop it! Stop this.
What kind of example are you both setting?"

That calmed Logan enough that he backed away,
clearly disgusted with himself for letting this self-
absorbed snob get to him. Then he turned to her, his
eyes blazing. "Do *you* want me and Caleb to go?"

She shook her head. "No. Of course not." Reaching a hand out to touch his arm, she said, "Logan,
you haven't done anything wrong."

Rad took her defense of Logan as a personal af-
front. Groaning loudly, he said, "Surely you aren't
going to let him stay on? The man attacked me, Tricia!"

Trixie whirled on him. "Yes, after you attacked his
son." Her tone firm, her eyes bright, she said, "Get
this through your head, Radford. I'm not going to sell
this ranch, and I'm not going to fire Logan."

Clearly frustrated, Rad threw up his hands. "I just don't get it. Ever since your father left you this stinking place, you've turned into Lady Bountiful. Are you so sure it's the land you want to hang on to, or do you still have a thing for him?"

He pointed to Logan, causing Logan to snarl and move toward Rad.

Before Logan could get very far, Harlan stepped forward, his bulky frame becoming an effective barrier between the two men. "I've had just about enough of this bickering between you two."

While the two men stared hotly at each other, Harlan said in a calm, authoritative tone, "Now, boys, this is the way it's gonna be. Tricia Maria is the sole owner of Brant Dunaway Farms International." Giving Rad a scathing glare, he continued, "She's made a firm decision to keep the ranch, and she's put Logan in charge of things in her absence. That's good enough for her ol' grandpa, so I say it's a done deal."

Turning to Logan, he said, "You, get a grip on that attitude. We're on your side, son." Then he frowned at Radford. "And you, get your tail back to Dallas and mind your own business. Trixie knows what she's doing."

His anger refueled, Rad glared hotly at Trixie. "Do you?"

"Yes, for the first time in a long time, I do," she replied quietly, her gaze shifting toward Logan.

An angry flush rose on Rad's face. "Well, we'll just see about that. I have some very influential friends, you know. I wonder how Social Services would react if I put the word out that your so-called foreman has a very dangerous temper?"

Dazed, Trixie could only stare at him in shock. "Rad, you can't be serious. You provoked him, and besides, we have witnesses to the whole thing. Stop spouting idle threats."

"Oh, it's no threat," Rad said, his expression smug. "And I'm telling you, Tricia, if he doesn't watch it, I'll call in all my markers."

Trixie put her hands on her hips, then turned to Logan. "I won't let that happen. Logan, you have my word on that."

Logan gave her a hostile look, then ran a hand through his tousled curls. "Sorry, but I can't go on your word right now, Trixie." His eyes shooting fire, his expression daring, he glared at Rad. "Do what you gotta do, but you stay away from my son. I've got things to take care of. See y'all in the morning."

Harlan watched him stalk away, then cleared his throat, his eyes on Rad. "I need a big glass of sweet tea to get this bitter taste out of my mouth. I'm going in the cookhouse to help Gayle tidy up."

That left Trixie and Rad in an uncomfortable silence.

Finally she looked over at him, her tone quiet, firm, and determined. "We need to talk."

He smirked. "I'll say. *You* need to come home with me right away. Do you realize you're acting so irresponsibly that you're seriously jeopardizing our whole relationship?"

She laughed bitterly at his twisted logic. Why had she never seen this shallowness in him before? Maybe because she hadn't wanted to see it? Maybe because it reflected a side of herself she didn't want to acknowledge?

"Oh, yes," she answered, "I realize a lot of things." Taking him by the hand, she led him toward the luxury rental car he'd parked out away from the main house. "I realize you have a nasty side that I don't like. I realize that you won't ever let me run this ranch the way I think it should be run. And I realize that, thanks to my mother's biased opinions, you hate Logan."

They made it to the car, and now Rad swung around to lean on the shiny gray metal, crossing his arms over his chest as he scowled at her. Ignoring her first two accusations, he went right to the heart of the matter. "Well, sure. You're engaged to me, yet you defended that…that hillbilly."

"He is not a hillbilly," she said, shaking her head. "Logan graduated from the University of Arkansas with a business degree and a minor in agriculture, and he's had training in youth counseling. He knows his stuff, but he does have a temper. You're lucky he didn't whip your pants off back there."

"All the more reason to press charges," he countered. "That man needs to be held accountable for his actions."

Frustrated, Trixie groaned, then threw her hands in the air. "Please, Rad, don't threaten Logan, or me, for that matter. If you did something irrational like that, you could very well close down this whole operation. And I won't let that happen. My father and Logan have worked too hard on this."

Rad stared down at her as if he were seeing her for the first time. Then, realization dawning in his self-involved system, he said, "You still care about him, don't you?"

Too tired to hide it any longer, she said, "Yes, Rad. Yes, I do. And that's one of the things I need to talk to you about."

Shaking his head, he gave her a patronizing chuckle. "No, no. You just need to come home. You can't think straight in this place." Pleading with her, he said, "We're engaged, remember? You're wearing my ring. I love you."

Trixie looked down at the perfect solitaire nestled on her finger, then lifted her gaze back to him. "No, Rad, you love the idea of being with me. You love us as the fashionable up-and-coming power couple around Dallas. You love our image, what we represent, and I have to admit, I once enjoyed all of that, too. But…now I understand things about myself…things I've tried to deny for so long. And you're right. I have changed since my father's death."

She hesitated, then took a deep breath. "You see, I've stepped out of my self-centered shell and I've taken a good hard look at my life. Seeing this ranch, knowing what my father tried to do here, has made me aware of the outside world, the world my mother has tried so hard to shield me from. But now that I've seen the work being done here, I think I want to be a part of all this." She lifted a hand to include the ranch. "I might be making a mistake, but I need to stay here awhile. I need to find some sort of peace."

"You're not making any sense," he said, impatient with all this soul searching.

Trixie gazed up at him, wishing, wishing they'd shared more intimate talks, wishing they'd shared a closer spirituality with each other. But now that she thought about it, she and Rad had never really had any heavy, meaningful conversations. No, they'd always been too busy seeing and being seen. Their whole relationship had been built on a carefully cultivated facade, orchestrated by Pamela to always put them in the best light.

Now Trixie wanted that facade to end. "Yes, Rad, I am making sense. Finally I'm taking charge of my own life." Touching a hand to his arm, she added, "And unfortunately, that means I can't marry you. It wouldn't be right now, because I don't love you anymore, not in the way I should."

He grew quiet then, his hand clinging tentatively to hers. "Because of him?"

"Yes, partly." She took another long, calming breath, then lifted up a prayer for strength. "But partly because something happened to me a few years ago, something that I've kept a secret from the world. And because of that, I can't love anyone completely. That's why I want you to know the truth.'"

He attempted a grin. "What'd you do, avoid paying your taxes or something?"

He would figure money into it. Rad just didn't have a clue as to any type of emotional depth. Which would make it even harder for him to understand what she was about to tell him.

"It has nothing to do with taxes," she began. "But, I did pay a high price for something. I...I used bad judgment, I suppose. I lost control and wasn't thinking straight, and...I paid dearly for it."

In an effort to soothe her, he placed a hand on each of her shoulders, his gaze full of affection and concern. "Tell me, honey. We'll work through it together, then things can go back to normal. I love you,

Tricia. We can handle all of this if you'll just come home with me.''

Wishing it were that simple, she touched a hand to his cheek. ''Rad, listen to me and try to understand what I'm saying. Eight years ago, I spent the night with a man and…and I got pregnant.''

Rad's breath hissed right out of his body. Slowly, as if he'd touched something filthy and distasteful, he dropped his hands away from her shoulders. ''What did you say?''

''I…was with a man once, and I got pregnant,'' she said again, her head down. Then lifting her gaze to his, she said, ''And I was forced to give the baby up for adoption. My mother and Brant and Harlan are the only ones who know. They made me agree to the adoption, and…I think we've all been in denial since.''

Rad stood silent, then. Trixie watched his face, saw the disgust and disapproval coloring his expression, much in the same way they'd colored her mother's face when she'd been forced to tell Pamela the truth years ago.

Oh, how it hurt to have to relive this all over again, especially with Rad. Yet, even through her hurt and humiliation, she felt an inner peace emerging to give her the strength to face him without shame. So she waited, hoping he'd show some compassion and at least try to understand.

Rad might not be good at intimacy or compassion, but he was good at numbers. It didn't take him long to put two and two together. ''It…it was him, right? You…you and Logan Maxwell?''

She flinched away from the look of utter revulsion

in his eyes. "Yes," she said, swallowing back the pain, the humiliation she'd worn for so long. She refused to be ashamed any longer, and she certainly wasn't ashamed of Logan. "He doesn't know about the baby, though. But I intend to tell him." *That* would be the hardest test.

Rushing on, she added, "We were only together that one time, then my parents made sure it would never happen again. Logan went on to college and, well, he was married briefly. They got divorced and now he has custody of their son, Caleb.

"That's why I can't sell the ranch. I won't displace that little boy, and I won't shut down a place where troubled teenagers can come and find hope. I've already lost one child because of everyone telling me I had no other choice. I won't do that to Logan and his child, or any other children who might need a temporary shelter here."

To her amazement, instead of condemning her, Rad laughed in relief. "Is that what this is all about? You think you owe Logan Maxwell something simply because you gave his bastard up for adoption! You're worse off than I thought!"

The slap sounded out over the hot, still dusk like a shutter flapping in a harsh whip of wind. Appalled at both Rad and herself, Trixie backed away, her stinging palm covering her mouth. The imprint of her hand spread like a bright red stain across Rad's stony face.

"I'm sorry," she said, shaken and heartbroken, all her hope for the last shreds of their shallow relationship dying with the final rays of the sun. Handing him the one-carat diamond ring he'd given her just months before, she said, "I think you'd better leave."

"Good idea," he retorted as he yanked open the car door. "I'll be glad to tell your mother the engagement is off." Before she could respond to that dig, he added, "Oh, and don't worry. Your tawdry little secret is safe with me. After all, I do have some dignity left, and I certainly don't want people to find out you dumped me for some low-life field hand who didn't even have the decency to acknowledge his indiscretion."

Fighting back tears, she repeated, "He never knew, Rad. But I'm going to tell him the truth before I leave here."

A triumphant smile crested on Rad's red streaked face. "Yeah, and then we'll see who's the better man. We'll see if Logan Maxwell will be so willing to work for you once he finds out you used your money and power to get rid of his baby. You're making a big mistake, but then, like Harlan so clearly pointed out—you're calling all the shots. I wish you lots of luck. You're going to need it."

"And lots of prayers, too," she whispered as she watched him pull away, the cruelty of his taunts tearing at her heart while she stood there in the dusty lane, her arms wrapped across her chest, her head bent.

In spite of Rad's callous observations, she managed to pull herself together. Lifting her head toward the afterglow of the setting sun, she sent up another prayer. And she decided she'd never be ashamed again.

Yes, she'd made a mistake, but now she was going

to get past that by dedicating her life to her father's work. Tonight she'd done something she should have done a long time ago. She'd told the truth. That gave her a very liberating feeling, as if a tremendous burden had been lifted from her shoulders.

As she strolled out toward the stables, she found a new sense of purpose. This was a turning point in her life, but this was only the beginning. Now she had to tell Logan the same thing she'd just told Rad. It was the only way to start fresh and find that second chance she needed so desperately. It was the only way to salvage the love she and Logan still had for each other.

She had set things in motion, and now she was willing to turn the rest over to God.

Hours later Logan watched and listened from his perch on the porch, worry creasing his brow as he waited for Trixie to come back. It was well past dark, and still no sign of her.

Would she come back? Or had dear, wonderful Radford, with all his charm and cunning, conned her into leaving with him?

And why, Logan wondered, did he care?

Because he loved her. In spite of everything, he still loved her. But would that be enough? Would his love carry them through when things got even tougher between them? Would he have the strength to lay it all on the line, to take a chance with her again? Or would he let his pride stand in the way once more?

The Bible said to trust in the Lord. He'd just had an evening devotional with the youth, his son at his side. Because of what had happened earlier, they'd

talked about accusation and anger, and how to control
the two.

"For his anger endureth but a moment; in his fa-
vour is life: weeping may endure for a night, but joy
cometh in the morning."

The verse from Psalms had hit the nail right on the
head, as Harlan had so tactfully pointed out before
he'd gone off to bed. Logan got the impression Harlan, and maybe the Lord, too, were both trying to hit
him on the head with something.

Was he too stubborn, too bitter, to get it?

He sat there in the rocking chair, listening to the
night sounds, trying so very hard to hear the echo of
his own wounded heart. He heard the moaning of the
humid wind as it merged with the gentle lowing of a
cow. A set of pewter wind chimes hanging from a
nearby rafter played a pretty, tinkling tune, its melody
telling him to forgive, forgive, live, live. The rich
smell of the earth mixed with the scent of fresh-baked
bread and the night dew. And off in the distance a
streak of lightning highlighted the starless sky. A
storm was coming across the Arkansas countryside.

Where was Trixie?

Torn between duty and need, Logan knew he
wouldn't have the strength to hold out much longer.
He wanted to tell her everything at last. He wanted
the answers to the questions that had haunted him for
eight long years. He wanted to put an end to the bitterness and the accusations, and the pain.

He wanted. He wanted to find joy in the morning.

His eyes misty with stubborn tears, he whispered
to the night. "There's so much, Lord. So much I need
to tell her...so much I need to ask her. She has her

secrets, and I have mine. I don't want any more secrets between us. I only ask for a second chance." His voice, his prayer trailed off into a humble plea. "I only want redemption."

The wind picked up. The chimes danced and jingled. The thunder grew closer.

And then the screen door squeaked open and Trixie stood there in her floral dress, her blond hair windswept and moon kissed, her eyes glistening like beckoning stars in the gray-black darkness.

"Logan?"

Logan hastily wiped his eyes, and without a word came up out of the creaking rocking chair to take her into his arms. Silently, softly, slowly, he pulled her to him. If he spoke now, he'd blurt everything out. And he needed time, time to collect himself, time to brace himself for what was to come.

Because when he told her the truth, he could very well lose her forever.

But not tonight. Not now. Tonight he only wanted to cherish the sweet victory of having her here still. Tonight he wanted to close the door on his conflicted soul and find that little bit of joy he felt each time she was in his arms. Tomorrow would be soon enough for the truth.

As a soft rain began to fall all around them, he held her close and waited and hoped and prayed.

And remembered.

"Weeping may endure for a night, but joy cometh in the morning."

Yes, in the morning he'd tell her everything.

And then he'd leave the rest up to God.

Chapter Ten

The storm worsened during the night, so the morning brought a whole new set of problems. While tornado watches prevailed across the state, heavy rains poured over the land, making the paddocks and pastures a muddy river of dirt and water. The animals huddled together, trying to find comfort and warmth in each other, while the humans went about their work in yellow rain slickers and heavy rubber boots. All across the ranch, pine limbs and oak branches lay broken and tangled, snapped from tall trees by the force of the winds.

Trixie took up residence in the office just off the den, where she called in to her own Dallas office to see if anything major had happened in the few days she'd been away on bereavement leave. Luckily her assistant and secretary were so efficient and organized that everything back in Dallas was well under control. Just a few questions to answer and some quick calls to clients, then Trixie was left to sit and watch the rain falling in spattering rivulets off the eaves of the wraparound porch.

Sipping another cup of strong coffee, she once again thought about everything that had happened to change her life over the past few days. She'd lost her father, inherited a ranch and found a part of herself that had been missing for a long time now. She was no longer engaged to Radford Randolph and—she was still in love with Logan Maxwell.

While those revelations summed things up in a nutshell, the complications of each resounded in her head like the rain hitting the shingles out on the slanted roof.

How would she ever find the courage to tell Logan the truth? And especially after last night, when he'd held her in his arms as if he never wanted to let her go. Finding him there on the porch, waiting for her to come home, had been just the balm her wounded soul had needed. He'd hugged her close, rocking his body against hers, soothing her with softly whispered endearments, then he'd turned and gone inside without another word between them.

Now, she couldn't help but remember Rad's condemning words. Would Logan be so forgiving, so willing to continue working here, once he found out the truth?

Sitting here now, in the worn leather chair where her father must have spent hours, she glanced around, savoring the spirit her father had left everywhere in the paneled, cluttered room, hoping to find the courage to face Logan again. Hoping he would be able to forgive her at last.

Honors and awards, plaques and belt buckles, were

displayed here and there, on every available surface. Professional Bull Riders Champion, 1977 and 1978. Rodeo Hall of Fame, 1994. PBR Ring of Honor—a circle of diamonds and gold, locked safely behind a glass case. National Finals Rodeo Champion, 1981. PRCA 1984 World Bull Riding Champion. The room was a testimony to Brant's love for the rodeo life, and his talent for riding the bulls.

Trixie sat back, closing her eyes as warm memories flooded through her mind. Her father had always been a cowboy. He'd never been interested in going into town with Harlan to learn the oil business. No, sir. No skyscrapers and silk suits for Brant Dunaway. Her father preferred mountains and mesquite trees to mergers and million-dollar deals. Brant could always be found out in the corrals and stables at Dunaway's Hideaway, riding, roping and hoping.

"From the time he was five years old…" Harlan said from the doorway now, as if reading his granddaughter's thoughts. "Your daddy sure loved riding those bulls and broncs."

Trixie opened her eyes, then sat up straight. "And mother hated it? Why?"

Harlan lowered his girth down onto a plaid wing chair nestled by a broad window. "Think about it, sugar. Bull riding is a very dangerous sport. Oh, she went to watch in the early days, when he was just setting out at every rinky-dink rodeo between Dallas and Oklahoma City. Pamela loved the romance, the glory, associated with being married to a handsome bull rider. But…one time, when you were about three years old and safe at home with your grandmama, God rest her soul, your ma watched your Daddy take a gore from a crazy-mad bull. Sliced through his gut and...well, he almost bled to death before they got him to the hospital. Had to remove his spleen.''

Trixie looked around the room at the many pictures of her father during his heyday. "I never knew."

"She didn't want you to know. And she spent the rest of their marriage trying to forget. That's why she hated what he did. Pamela was so afraid he'd get killed."

Marveling at all the undercurrents she'd never been aware of in her parent's relationship, Trixie said, "So she did love him."

"Still loves him."

"But why did she drive him away?"

Harlan shook his head. "She nagged him away. Brant was a proud man. He wasn't about to let a goring stop him from becoming the best he could be. And he surely wasn't going to let a worrisome wife turn him into a coward."

Trixie scowled at that. "Men and their pride."

Harlan countered, "Women and their demands."

"Expectations," she corrected. "We have high expectations, and sometimes—"

"Sometimes a man can't live up to that kind of pressure," her grandfather finished for her. Changing the subject with a briskness that equaled the wind outside, he asked, "Did Rad live up to your expectations?"

"No," she said, lowering her head to stare at a photograph of her father with little Caleb on his knee. A shard of pain and longing hit her as she gazed at the framed picture. Brant had lost his own family;

he'd turned to Logan's son for comfort, she supposed. And somewhere out there...

She refused to think about the child she would never know. Instead, she looked up at her grandfather. "Rad and I broke up last night."

Harlan nodded, then said, "Well, now you can 'dance with the one who brung you.'"

"And what's that supposed to mean?"

"You and Logan," he said, rising up with a huffing breath. "You two have some unsettled business between you, I believe. And I say, now's the time to settle it."

"What if it's too late?" she asked, the hope in her voice edged with fear.

"It's never too late, if you tell the truth and trust in the Lord."

"I'm trying, Granddaddy. I'm trying."

Harlan leaned his meaty hands against the burgundy leather desk pad. "Tricia Maria, I know we don't speak about what happened much—heck, we never talk about it. But I want you to know that...that I'm sorry I didn't fight harder for you back then."

Trixie stood up to come around the desk. Hugging her grandfather close, she said, "I certainly don't blame you. You were up against both Mother and Daddy, same as me. I just wish—"

"Me, too," he said, his eyes misty and full of regret. "I wish a whole lot of things. Maybe that's why I'm so determined to see that you and Logan at least try to get things straight between the two of you."

Patting him on the back, she said, "I plan on telling him...everything, as soon as I can work up my nerve. Where is he this morning, anyway?"

"Out rounding up stock and cleaning up debris, I imagine," Harlan said. "That weather turned nasty during the night. Fences down, trees blown over. Frightened animals to tend. The rancher's life is a tough one, even on good days, but Logan will get things under control."

"He's a lot like Daddy, isn't he?"

"Yep. He's stubborn and prideful, but determined to do his best."

She stared at the rain for a minute, then said, "Rad isn't like that. He only does what he has to do to make the best possible impression. It was never real between us. It was all carefully calculated, all part of the overall plan. Even his feelings for me were superficial and based on what he could gain from being with me. And I'm ashamed to admit it, but I felt the same way toward him. He was the perfect choice, so I went along with it." Shrugging, she added, "I almost made another mistake, didn't I?"

"You stopped it in time," Harlan replied, then winked. "'Course, your ma will be fit to be tied."

"I'll deal with her," Trixie assured him. "I do believe it's high time I stood up to her."

"That's the spirit. You've got a lot of your ol' daddy in you, Trixiebelle."

"Thanks, Granddaddy," she said as she waved him out of the office. Somehow, in spite of the dreary day, in spite of her breakup with Rad, she did feel stronger.

Maybe being here, amidst her father's things, helped. Maybe knowing Logan still loved her helped. But would he still love her when she told him everything?

Just then the door creaked open and Trixie found

herself staring at a pint-sized set of six-guns. Playing along, she raised her hands. "Oh, my. Am I being held up by a bandit?"

Caleb sauntered into the room, dressed in brown imitation chaps and his ever-present cowboy hat. "Yes, ma'am," he said in his best cowboy drawl. "I come to take all your valuables."

Pretending to be frightened, Trixie waved a hand. "Please, take whatever you'd like, sir. I don't want to get shot down in my mangy tracks."

Caleb giggled, then put his dangerous looking fake weapons on the desk. "I ain't gonna shoot you, Miss Trixie. Mr. Brant taught me guns are for hunting, not killing people."

"He told you that, did he?" she asked as she scooped the little boy up on her lap. He smelled of life, all warm and sweaty, with just a trace of sugar cookie lingering around him like a halo. "Mr. Brant was a very wise man."

"Yeah, and he was smart, too," Caleb replied with big-eyed innocence. "He taught me how to ride, you know?"

"Did he now?" Trixie's heart went all soft and mushy at the thought of her father patiently teaching little Caleb all about the rodeo. "But not those nasty old bulls, I hope?"

"Sure I want to ride bulls, just like him," Caleb answered, looking at her as if she'd just fallen off the turnip truck. "But I like the broncs, too."

"Even worse," she said, her hand touching tentatively on his back. "A very dangerous sport."

He shrugged. "Girls always say that. Nana thinks the same way."

"Nana's about as smart as Mr. Brant," Trixie replied, afraid to move, afraid he'd run off into his fantasy land again and leave her here to deal with reality. It just felt so nice, so special, to be holding a child in her lap.

Caleb sighed long and hard, then dropped his shoulders. "He was your Daddy, huh?"

She smiled at the boy's sweet innocence. "Yes, he was. I didn't get to see him very much, since I lived so far away. But he was still my Daddy."

Caleb grew quiet then. When he looked up at her, his eyes were wide and completely honest. "I miss him."

"Me, too," Trixie said, her voice barely above a whisper. "He was a special man."

Caleb lifted a finger to point to the ring nestled in a velvet box behind the glass case. "Know what? He told me he'd give me that ring one day. Told me I ought to have it."

Surprised that Brant would be willing to part with such a prestigious and valuable award, she looked down at the little boy. "Are you sure it was that particular ring?"

Caleb bobbed his head, causing his hat to tip back. "Oh, yeah. His Ring of Honor. He told me only real all-around rodeo cowboys could wear that ring."

She smiled down at him, thinking she'd never seen a cuter cowboy in her life. And she'd seen a few in her time. "Well, you certainly are a real all-around cowboy, aren't you?"

His nod was swift and confident. "Yep. I'm gonna be the best. I'm gonna be just like Mr. Brant."

Realizing her father and this precious little boy

must have had a special relationship, Trixie once more pushed back the hurt of never knowing her own child. Brant should have been able to share things with his own grandchild, but none of them had taken the time to think about that back when they were so concerned about the Dunaway name and position. Instead they'd hurriedly sent her child away, in the name of maintaining the family status and dignity. Lord, would she never be able to forgive herself?

Staring down at Caleb now, she said, "I promise you—one day you will have that ring."

"Okay," he said as he shoved off her lap, his trust in her as complete as the few minutes of quiet he'd spent here in this room. "Mr. Brant said when I grow up and prove myself, then I can have it." He twisted his face in a confused grimace. "What do you have to do to prove yourself, anyway?"

Trixie shifted in the chair, feeling empty now. "Well," she said, her eyes focused on the little boy waiting for an answer, "you have to be honest and hardworking, and you have to care about other people and…you have to always respect others as well as yourself." Sighing, she added, "Sometimes, proving yourself is a tough job."

He grinned then. "I can do all of that. My daddy's proved himself a whole bunch, 'cause he does all of that stuff."

Trixie's smile was bittersweet. Maybe it was time she proved herself, too. It would be worth it, just to win Caleb's praise. And Logan's. "Your daddy is a special man."

"Just like Mr. Brant was," Caleb reminded her. Then, in typical cowboy fashion, he tugged his battered hat low over his brow and gave her a determined look. "I want that ring. I'm gonna work hard, I promise."

It was a long time before Trixie could reply. "Then it's a deal."

"What's a deal?" Logan said from the door.

Trixie looked up to find his dark eyes centered on her, that worried look she'd come to recognize and dread moving like a thunderstorm across his damp, mud-smudged face. He looked so powerful, so all male, standing there in his heavy twill rain duster, with his hat dripping water, that she had to agree with little Caleb. Logan had more than proven himself. He'd saved this ranch. And maybe her, too.

"It's a secret," Caleb said, turning to Trixie for support in this new game.

"Yes, a special secret," Trixie replied, amused by the wary look in Logan's eyes. "Don't worry, we're not planning anything illegal or illicit."

"What's ill—illis—it?" Caleb asked.

Trixie laughed then. "It means something underhanded and shifty. But not you—you're not in trouble."

"Not yet, anyway," Logan said, relaxing a little bit. "Scoot off to the kitchen and get you some beef stew, sport."

Caleb picked up his guns and rushed past his father, but not before Logan grabbed his hat and tousled his hair a little bit.

"He's so cute, Logan," she said, nervous now that she was alone with him again. "And smart as a whip."

He watched her for a minute, the hesitant expression on his face telling her more than words ever could. Trixie waited, half expecting him to say something, to tell her what was on his mind. But the blankness returned, curtaining his feelings like the gray clouds outside, hovering, moving, misting over whatever he'd been about to say.

"That's my boy," he replied finally, lifting a shoulder off the doorjamb. "Hope he wasn't filling your head with tall tales."

"No, just telling me he wants to be a bull rider."

Logan's grin was weak with worry. "Yeah, we're still negotiating that matter." He took off his slicker, then sat down. In a quiet voice he said, "Your father was his hero."

"So I gathered."

They sat for a minute, staring, very much aware of each other, the rain, falling more gently now, the only sound between them.

Finally Logan said, "Hey, I was wondering…I mean, when this bad weather is over and…I've got some free time…I was wondering if we could get together and maybe get away from here for a couple of hours."

Touched by his invitation and his nervousness, Trixie lifted her brow and said, "Are you asking me out on a date, Logan?"

He tugged his hat off, ran a hand through his damp curls, then sighed long and hard, the glint in his dark eyes taking her breath away. "Yep. I guess you could call it that."

She ruffled some papers on the desk to hide her own jitters. Getting away from the ranch for a quiet talk would be better for her, too. She could tell him what she needed to say without any interruptions. ''That would be…nice.''

He pulled himself out of the chair then, his hat in his hands, his gaze on hers. ''It's just…we need to talk, about the ranch, about us, about everything.''

Trixie stood, too, mostly to keep busy, her hands in her shorts pockets. ''I agree. I guess you figured out I broke up with Rad last night.''

She saw the relief in his eyes. But she also saw something else—that same wariness she'd witnessed so many times, over the past few days. Well, it was only natural for him to be on guard around her. They had a highly intimate history. She was still treading lightly around him herself.

''I can't say I'm sorry,'' he admitted, tipping his head to one side as he gazed over at her. ''He was a first-class—''

''Careful,'' she warned, her smile a little sad, a little happy. ''Remember, you have to set a good, upstanding example for the young people.''

''Yeah, right.'' He nodded, then turned to leave, his long slicker hooked with a thumb over his shoulder and floating out behind him. ''See you at lunch.''

''I'll be there.'' Then, ''Logan, do you need any help?'' She motioned toward the window. ''It's so bad out there—I could ride fences or check on those adorable piglets.''

He grinned, then shook his head. ''Nope. You just stay here and keep Mama company…until I get back. She could use a hand with Caleb. He gets kinda restless when he can't play outside.''

''All right.''

''All right. See you later.''

Trixie waited until he'd stomped down the hall before hugging her arms to her chest, thankful that Logan didn't seem to mind her being around Caleb so much anymore.

Then a terrible thought occurred to her. Would he want her around his son once she told him the truth?

Would he ever want her again, once he found out she'd given up his child without even telling him?

By the end of the day Trixie did get to go out and help with the cleanup work. In fact, every available hand was needed in order to corral skittish animals and secure broken fences. The electricity had gone out during the afternoon, so she couldn't get much work done in the office, anyway. She'd spent most of her time trying to entertain Caleb while his grandmother had gone about her regular daily chores. The little boy had stolen her heart, much in the same way his father had when she'd first met him.

Then, leaving Gayle to man the cellular phones and feed the workers cold sandwiches, she headed out with Logan and Caleb in the misting rain.

Cloaked in a bright yellow slicker and a rain hat, she rode a docile mare around the perimeter of the corrals, checking one last time for strays or places in the fence they might have missed earlier. Off in the distance, she could hear the four-wheeler revving up. Samantha would take the lane and check the far pastures before dark set in.

Up ahead, riding with his father on Rocky, Caleb shouted to Samantha as she whizzed by. "Can I come?"

Samantha slowed the four-wheeler down, then

lifted a questioning hand to Logan. "I don't mind, if you don't."

Logan stared down at his son, then seeing the hopeful expression on Caleb's face, nodded. "Go ahead. I'm too tired to argue with you." As Caleb scrambled down to race to the off-road vehicle, Logan called, "And put on that helmet stashed under the seat!"

Samantha saw to it that the boy followed his father's instructions, then with Caleb sitting firmly on the wide seat with her, headed slowly off down the lane.

"He loves to ride that thing," Logan replied as Trixie coaxed her horse up beside his. "He's been begging me to let him drive it, but I haven't had time to teach him."

"He's certainly all boy," Trixie replied, as glad to be out of the house as Caleb, even if it was still a nasty day. "You've done a good job with him, Logan."

He glanced over at her, his eyes lifting underneath the brim of his hat. "Mama's helped out there a lot."

Noticing that cautious, guarded look in his eyes again, Trixie said, "It must have been hard on you—after your wife left, I mean."

Logan looked straight ahead, his face as blank and stony as the weathered posts of the wire fence stretching out beside them. "It was. Donna and I met in our first year of college...right after—"

"Right after you and I," she finished, understanding dawning in her eyes, regret pooling in her heart. "You must have really fallen for her."

He grunted. "I didn't fall at all. I didn't really love her the way I should have. Oh, I thought I loved her.

I wanted to love her. But—'' He stopped, looked off into the distance, his eyes swirling with the same dark intensity as the clouds curling and churning over the horizon. Then with a hard, cold look that left her breathless and afraid, he pinned Trixie. ''I was still so in love with you, I couldn't think straight. So I used her to ease the pain. I cared about her, and I needed her. But, she knew. She always knew. So she left me.''

And her child. Shocked, Trixie stared over at him. If this were some sort of declaration, it didn't make her feel any better, knowing she'd caused so much heartache. The condemning look in his eyes contrasted sharply with the gentleness she'd seen in him last night, only adding to her confusion and her fears.

''You still resent me, don't you?'' she said, hurt in spite of her understanding. She didn't dare chastise his ex-wife for leaving Caleb. She'd done no better herself, after all. ''Why, Logan?''

He couldn't tell her exactly why he resented her even while he loved her, so he only nodded and said, ''I resent a lot of things. I resent your money and your mother. I resent your indifference to your father. But mostly, Tricia Maria, I just regret…so much.''

They'd reached a small copse of trees at the corner of one of the pastures. Having seen no fences that needed his immediate attention, Logan slipped off his horse then turned to Trixie.

Before he could touch her, though, she dropped down and tied the mare's reins to a low branch, more intent on getting some much-needed answers than making sure her animal was secure.

Her eyes blazing blue fire, she said, ''Logan, you're

a constant contradiction. One minute you tell me you still love me, then the next you seem so distant, so bitter I can't reach you at all. What's going on?''

Tired, frustrated, yearning, Logan pulled her into his arms, his hands knocking her hat off so he could pull her head up. "You," he said, the one word half endearing, half hateful. "You—coming back here to stake a claim on everything from my heart to the ground I'm standing on. I've fought against you for so long, Trixie. I've blocked you out of my mind all these years, for reasons I can't even begin to explain now, and yet, here you stand. Here you are, in my arms, where I've always dreamed you should be. And I want you…I've prayed for you to be mine, but—"

"But?" She saw the torment in his eyes, saw the disgust on his face. He was fighting a battle, against her, against himself. "What is it? What did I do that was so terrible?"

He looked away, his grip on her still firm and sure, even if the doubt in his eyes told her he wasn't so sure. "You gave up," he said simply.

Wanting him to understand, she placed her hands on his face, the roughness of his five-o'clock shadow grating the nerve endings on her fingers. "Logan, I wanted to stay here with you. I wanted…"

She couldn't tell him she'd wanted nothing more than to come to him and tell him she was having his child. She'd wanted nothing more than to marry him and raise that child here on this ranch with him. But, ashamed, confused, humiliated—and taunted by her mother's hateful, insinuating words—she *had* given in and given up. Too soon. Too late.

And how, dear God, was she supposed to tell him

the truth now, when he still seemed so torn whenever he looked at her or touched her? The truth would turn him away forever, no matter how much he loved her.

"Do you love me now, Logan?" she asked, her hands on his face urging him to look at her. "Do you love me right this minute?" She had to know, had to take what little she could find. "Look at me and tell me the truth."

He did, his eyes locking with hers, his heart breaking with loyalty and honor, and his love for her. "Yes," he said. "I love you."

She was crying now. She had to tell him. She had to let go of all of the pain and the heartache, and she would make him understand somehow. But first...

"I love you," she said, her hands stroking the hard lines of his jaw. "I never stopped loving you, and...in my own way, I was using Rad just like you said you used Donna. We've both been playing these games, the games other people expect us to play. I left you because I had no choice, no choice. My mother made me feel dirty, sinful, full of contempt for myself. And since then I've prayed to God to forgive me, to forgive me for everything." She stopped, her breath hitching between sobs. "I did more than leave the man I loved. I gave up everything, Logan. Everything."

He waited, holding his breath, his eyes never leaving hers, the expectation, the anticipation on his face making him look harsh and hopeful all at the same time. "Tell me about it, Trixie. I really want to understand."

Oh, how she wanted to do that very thing. How she wanted to unburden herself to him, to tell him the horrible, honest truth at last. Would she find her redemption then, she asked the heavens. Or would she just be alone all over again, without any forgiveness or compassion?

Something in his eyes told her to trust him, to trust herself, to trust God. It was almost as if Logan knew all of her secrets and yet wanted to hear them from her lips just to confirm the strength of their love.

Impossible. He didn't know. He couldn't know. He just thought she'd dumped him because she was shallow and afraid. And maybe that had been true once, but not now. Not anymore.

Because she loved him so much, because she knew she might not ever get another chance, she pulled his head down and kissed him with a tender urgency, needing to feel his lips on hers just once more, needing to know that he loved her for this moment, in this place, standing here on this land. Just once more.

"I love you, Logan," she said after lifting her mouth from his. "Please remember that. I love you." Then she stepped back, distancing herself from him, from the pain. "And because I do love you, I want you to know the truth."

Logan let out a deep, shuddering sigh, then dropped his hand away from her hair. "I have some things to tell you, too." His eyes went soft again, then he trailed a finger down her cheek. "But you first."

Trixie hitched another breath. "We were supposed to do this over a candlelight dinner."

"We've got the rain and the wind," he said. "And the darkness."

She shook her head. "I've been in the dark too long now. It's time to come out into the light."

"Then come on," he said. "I'll find some candles and a dry spot."

She took his hand, ready to face the sure knowledge that he would soon hate her all over again. Ready to test her faith and their love for each other.

That's when they both heard the roar of an engine off in the distance, followed by a crash.

And after that, all they could hear was a long, keening scream.

Chapter Eleven

Everything after that became a nightmarish haze to Trixie, a shock-filled, dreamlike groping to see clearly, and to remember. She remembered running, running to her horse, with Logan close on her heels. She remembered galloping down the lane, toward the place from where the sounds, the horrible, telling sounds, had come.

And then, hours later, as she sat in the cold, sterile hospital waiting room, she had to put her hands to her face to block out the sight of little Caleb lying so still, so silent, in the mud of a shallow rocky ravine, with blood, so much blood, coming from the split on the side of his skull while the overturned four-wheeler's tires moved, spinning, spinning to nowhere.

She closed her eyes, trying to stop the inevitable tears, trying to block the memory of the stark terror on Logan's face as he scrambled down the slope to reach his son. How could she ever forget the way he'd bent over his child, unable to take Caleb in his arms for fear of hurting him worse, one hand tentatively touching the deep cut on Caleb's head as Logan told him over and over, "It'll be all right. It'll be all right. Daddy's here."

And Daddy had done all the right things, in spite of his own shock. Logan had administered CPR like a pro; he'd been trained for just such an accident. Once he was sure Caleb wasn't hurt anywhere else and that no apparent bone fractures existed, he'd carefully checked the head wound, cautious not to make it bleed even more. But because Caleb was unconscious, they all knew the seriousness of the situation. Still, somehow, Logan had remembered what to do.

So much to remember, so much had changed in one split second of tragedy.

Samantha had come running, tears falling down her face, mud streaking her clothes. "He...I got off to check on a lamb. We saw it down in the ravine...we heard it crying. I thought it might be hurt. He...Caleb stayed on the vehicle. He'd taken his helmet off to...to scratch his head. His head was itching."

Trixie had held the girl, trying to calm her, trying to put the image of that sweet, still little body out of her mind. "What happened, Samantha?"

"I...I think he tried to drive the four-wheeler. I heard the engine. I turned around and..." The girl held a fist to her trembling lips. "It just took off, shot off right into the ditch. Caleb flew through the air and...he hit his head on those rocks." Falling against Trixie, she said, "Oh, Miss Trixie, I'm so sorry. What have I done?"

"Shhh," Trixie had said, soothing, touching, her

gestures nervous and erratic as she'd watched Logan moving like a zombie up the shallow, muddy incline. "It's not even that deep here. How could…?"

She'd let go of Samantha to walk slowly toward Logan, her eyes searching his face, her heart dropping with the weight of fear and dread. How could she ever forget the look on his face, so cold, so stony, so… accusing. "Logan?"

He didn't answer her. He just keep walking, faster now, never stopping until he'd reached his horse. With a walkie-talkie he pulled from his saddle bag, he radioed Harlan back at the house and told him in a clipped, calm voice to call 911. Then he slid back down into the ditch, doing what he could for his son.

Horrified, Trixie stared down at the scene, her arms hugging her chest as she watched Logan carefully cushion his son's neck with a rolled-up saddle blanket for support. Then he covered Caleb with his heavy twill duster.

The tiny hand Logan touched with his bigger hand drooped like a broken feather. In spite of Logan's calm, reassuring words, Caleb's eyes remained closed. His face, so pale and serene, looked, other than the bright red spot of blood congealing at the base of his skull, like that of a sleeping angel.

"Logan?" She realized she sounded panicky and frantic, but she rushed down to him, oblivious to the mud and slippery rocks, pulling Samantha along with her. "Logan, please, tell me—is he still—"

"He's alive," Logan growled, his words low and full of a misery she would never, ever be able to forget. "We…*I* have to get him to the hospital."

With that, he turned away, giving all of his attention back to his son.

"I'm coming with you," she said as she fell down beside him, her eyes on the little boy lying between them.

Logan didn't look at her or answer her. He just sat there holding on to his son, willing the little boy to hang on, his whispered encouragements becoming more and more urgent with each moment.

Trixie thought she would go insane with the waiting. Time seemed to stop. It seemed as if the whole ranch stilled, waiting, hoping. The rain slowed to a fine, silent mist. The air was still as the minutes slid slowly by. The only sound was that of water dripping off the yellow-green leaves of nearby trees.

"Where are they?" Logan finally asked, the impatience in his voice tempered with a hint of fear as he checked Caleb's pulse yet again.

Finally, off in the distance, they heard the screaming sirens crashing through the still silence, the urgency of their whine only mirroring the urgent scream inside Trixie's pounding head.

"I'm coming with you," she repeated, her eyes searching Logan's face.

He whirled, the look he shot her full of venom and anger. "No."

"Logan?" Her whole body trembled with fear, with a tragic sickening. "Logan, I want to help you."

He didn't answer her. Instead, Logan hopped up, motioning with waving arms to the approaching ambulance. Then he rushed toward the paramedics, explaining what had happened, the urgency of the situation his only focus now. He ignored Gayle's frantic calls as she jumped out of the ambulance cab and ran toward them; he ignored everything and everyone except his son. He waited, letting the experts do their stuff, then he followed them as they hurriedly lifted the stretcher into the ambulance, then he hopped in after them without a word to anyone.

Trixie watched, her heart shattering, when Logan once again took his son's hand and began crooning softly to him. With a look of hope and a gentle touch to his son's forehead, he wrapped the fresh blanket the emergency crew had provided over Caleb's body.

Gayle climbed into the ambulance with Logan before Trixie could. When she would have protested, both Gayle and Logan glared at her with such a harsh, pronouncing statement, she backed away, her hands to her mouth, her eyes filling with tears.

They were both obviously too distraught for her to argue with them right now. Besides, Caleb belonged to them; they had every right to be there with him. While she, she was an outsider who had no right, no reason to ride in that ambulance. Except that she cared.

"We'll take your car," Samantha said, seeing the worry on Trixie's face. The youth counselor became the calm one now, the one who knew what had to be done. "C'mon, Miss Trixie. Just let me leave someone in charge of the other kids. I'll get one of the adult volunteers."

She rushed off, her braids flowing out behind her.

Then Harlan pulled up, jumped out of his car and came trudging up the lane, surprise and concern etching his wrinkled face. "What in the world? Logan didn't give me all the details, and I'm too old to make this long walk in a hurry.''

He took one look at Trixie's face and placed both arms on hers to steady her. ''What's happened, girl?''

Trixie swallowed, shuddered, fell into his open embrace. ''Caleb—he had an accident on the four-wheeler. He…he won't wake up. Granddaddy, he won't wake up.''

''Let's go,'' Harlan said, not even stopping to get his Stetson. After convincing Samantha to stay on the ranch with the other frightened children, he insisted on driving, since Trixie was too shaken to maneuver the slippery highways.

So now here she sat, in a corner, in the cold, condemning lights of a sharp-angled, steel-encased waiting room. Waiting. Waiting.

It seemed she'd been waiting for something, someone, since the day she'd left another hospital's maternity ward so long ago. Now she only wanted Caleb to wake up and tell her that he was the best all-around cowboy in the world. *Just that one thing, Lord,* she prayed over and over again. *Just let him be all right.*

It didn't matter right now that Logan was as distant and cold as he'd been the day she'd returned to the ranch. It didn't matter that Gayle sat dry-eyed and silent, her eyes staring straight ahead, her expression grim. It didn't matter that she couldn't break through their pain, their hostility, except to know that they were hurting, afraid, dreading what the doctor might tell them any minute.

Trixie wanted to offer comfort; indeed, she'd tried. But Logan had only pushed her away. She had the sinking feeling that he blamed her, because he'd been with her at the time of the accident. But right now she didn't care about that. Right now she only wanted Caleb to be all right.

She got up to try again. Logan stood looking out a huge window at the end of the hall, his hands braced so tightly against the window frame, she could see the white of his hair-dusted knuckles underneath his permanent tan.

"Logan?"

"Not now," he snarled without even turning to see her.

She wanted to touch him, wanted to hold him close and promise him that Caleb would pull through, but his rejection pressed at her and tore through her, making her see that in spite of how much he claimed to love her, he was still holding back from her. He couldn't share this with her, because he still wasn't ready to let her be a part of his life.

Telling herself that now wasn't the time to wallow in self-pity, she sat back down. Now…now she had to concentrate on praying for Caleb. Now she had to be strong and quiet, for Logan's sake. Soon, Caleb would be just fine, and she and Logan could have that long talk they'd wanted to have. They could whisper by candlelight and make plans for the ranch and for…

For what? she had to ask herself, the glaring reality of her secret sin shouting down the efficient hallway at her. Did she really believe she could have a future with Logan? They'd never really gone beyond admitting their love for each other. And today, just when they were making progress, this terrible tragedy had happened to remind them that they'd always been dangerous for each other. What now? What next?

What if Caleb didn't make it?

She heard the doors from the examining room open. Dr. James Arnold, the neurologist assigned to Caleb's case, came marching out of the set of double doors leading from the operating room down the hallway, his face stern, his eyes guarded and dark with knowledge and secrets.

Logan turned, his gaze sweeping over the doctor, his hand reaching out. "Tell me," he said, his voice raw, his words a rasp.

Dr. Arnold, tall, with a thick head of wispy brown hair, stood with his hands behind his sterile hospital scrubs. "I'm not going to beat around the bush with you, Mr. Maxwell. Your son suffered a traumatic head wound, but the good news is—the brain wasn't affected as badly as we first thought. His wounds were serious, though—there was some swelling in the brain. We found a small blood clot, so we had to fix that to relieve the pressure."

"Surgery?" Gayle said, her hand going to her heart. Because her son couldn't bring himself to ask it, she did. "Will…will there be any…brain damage?"

Trixie closed her eyes, willing, praying, telling herself that couldn't happen. That just could not happen.

The doctor's features softened, but the look in his eyes was honest. "It's too soon to tell. In a perfect world, the swelling will go down and the brain will mend on its own. And little Caleb will wake up and be fine."

Logan turned with a grunt and hit the edge of his

fist against the side of a soft-drink machine, the echo of his frustration and helpless rage resounding down the hallway.

Rubbing his throbbing hand, he said, "But this isn't a perfect world, is it, Doc? And you can't tell me that my little boy is going to be the same when he wakes up. You can't even tell me if he's going to live or die."

Dr. Arnold didn't reprimand Logan, but he didn't back down, either. "Hope springs eternal, Mr. Maxwell."

Logan's laugh was bitter and hard edged. "Yeah, right. Hope. There's always hope, isn't there?" He looked around then, at his mother, at Trixie, at Harlan. "I've been clinging to hope for so long...I'm tired, you know? Just plain tired." Then, he stepped close, his face inches from the doctor's, his eyes bright with tears he refused to allow or acknowledge. "But, I'll tell you this. I won't give up on that little boy in there." He pointed down the hall, toward the ominous looking double doors, toward the room where his child lay. "I won't give up on him. You see, he's the only thing I've got left."

The doctor took Logan's impassioned declaration in stride. He'd seen it before so many times. "The power of hope," he said, his voice low and filled with compassion, "the power of prayer, Mr. Maxwell, can sometimes move mountains that mere doctors have to walk away from. I could use your help with that." He looked around the small group. "All of you."

Trixie never thought she could hurt any worse. She'd thought giving her own child away had been the worst pain imaginable, but she'd been wrong, so wrong. Watching Logan now, seeing him go through this terrible grief, this waiting, this not knowing, was killing her slowly and softly. Well, she wasn't going to let it happen.

Without a word she stalked down the hall, intent on finding the hospital chapel.

Harlan rushed after her, his old eyes haggard with worry. "Where you going, child?"

"To pray," she said simply.

Her grandfather nodded, then turned back to comfort Gayle.

When Trixie turned at the elevator, she saw Logan staring at her, his expression harsh and hard, unyielding. Whatever resentment and bitterness he felt toward her, whatever silent, secret pain he now suffered, she understood. And for once in her life, for once, somehow, she intended to make things right.

She'd pray Caleb well.

And then she'd get as far away from Logan as possible.

Because she could never, ever put him through this kind of hurt again.

Which meant she couldn't possibly tell him the truth.

Logan stood by his son's bed, holding one tiny hand in his bigger one, hoping that little bit of contact would bring Caleb out of his unconscious state. He couldn't help but relive the nightmare of the past few hours, couldn't help but take on the guilt of not being there when his son had needed him the most.

No, instead, he'd been kissing Tricia Maria Dunaway, and pledging his undying love to her yet again. And again that love had cost him.

His son was in a coma.

Maybe it was time he just told her the truth.

He wanted to blame someone; might as well be Trixie. After all, he'd certainly blamed her all of these years, and he was sure blaming her right this minute. Why not just go ahead and get it all out of his system?

Would that save his son?

Would that save his soul?

Holding Caleb's hand tightly in his, he talked in a low, shaky voice. "There's so much, son," he began, wishing, hoping he could find the courage to see this through. "There's so much I need to tell you. Do you know how much your Daddy loves you? Do you?"

The little body didn't move a muscle. The eyes remained closed behind the lush brown lashes. Caleb's face looked so peaceful, so calm, while his father's whole body screamed with a silent, taut tension that begged to be released.

"C'mon, Caleb," he tried again, determination willing the hitch in his voice to go away. "Wake up, cowboy. Gotta get back up on that horse. Isn't that what your…isn't that what Brant used to tell you when you fell down and skinned your knee?"

Logan stopped, waiting, watching, his eyes misting over in spite of his resolve not to cry. With a stubborn swipe of the back of his hand across his face, he dashed the tears away. "Courage, son. Courage. And I don't mean the kind where you act the fool. I mean real courage. You don't have to be a bull rider, son. Not for me." Gripping Caleb's hand, rubbing his son's arm with his other hand, he added, "All you have to do is find the courage to wake up. Just wake up, Caleb.''

Courage. The one word resounded like an echo through Logan's frazzled brain. Here he stood, demanding, begging, his son to wake up, when he himself had been asleep for so long. Did he have the right to teach Caleb about courage, when he'd never known the meaning of the word himself?

Gayle came into the room then, her eyes red rimmed, her expression wilted and tired. ''Let me sit with him a spell,'' she said, dismissing her son with a pat on the arm. ''I'll call you right away if he wakes up, I promise.''

Logan nodded, then turned to face his mother. ''I do need to take care of something.''

''Logan?'' she asked, her eyes lifting to her son's, frightened and filled with worry.

''I have to do it, Mama,'' he replied, knowing her question before she even asked it. ''It's high time I own up to my responsibilities.''

Gayle didn't try to stop him. Instead, she touched a hand to his hair, lifting the wispy strains away from his forehead much in the same way she'd done when he was young. ''I think you're right. Maybe it is time to let go of all the lies and the heartache.''

Lies and heartache. Trixie sat in the quiet hospital chapel, a small, square room with a white altar, mauve silk flowers and soft lightning. A room full of peace and calm, a beacon for all the confused souls that came screaming and shouting to God in their time of need.

Did God listen to someone like her? she had to

wonder. Did He answer the prayers of the unworthy, of those who'd only brought lies and heartache with them to his altar?

"I'm asking You now, God," she said, her head lifting to the stained-glass window rising over the altar. "I'm not asking for myself, but for Caleb. I'm asking You to make him better, to help him to wake up."

She sat silent for a minute, groping for an answer. "This child…this child means so much to his father, to his grandmother, to me. Please, Lord, let him be okay. Just let him be all right."

From the back of the room, Trixie heard a noise. Twisting in her spot on one of the smooth wooden pews, she turned to see Logan standing there, the double doors swinging behind him. The look on his face, that look of torment and dread she'd seen so many times these past few days, was evident as he stalked toward her.

"Where were you?" he asked, anger pulsating through every vein of his body. "Where were you, Tricia Maria, when Caleb needed you the most?"

Thinking he was angry with her because he'd been with her when Caleb got hurt, she lifted her gaze to him. "I'm sorry, Logan. I know you feel guilty for not being there when…when Caleb took off in the four-wheeler—"

"Yeah, I feel guilty. You're right about that. I shouldn't have turned my back, but I did. For you. Always for you. But I'm not talking about what happened today, Trixie."

Trying to find some measure of calm amidst her

confusion, she asked, "Then what are you talking about?"

Logan pushed his way to her to stand over her, then he pointed an accusing finger in her face. "I'm talking about what happened between us eight years ago. I mean, where were you when he was a baby? Where were you when he had to be fed in the middle of the night? When he cut his first tooth? When he learned to walk?"

A stunning, sickening realization poured through Trixie's entire system. Even as the magnitude of Logan's condemning questions swept through her, she brought her hands up to her mouth, then shook her head in denial. "I don't know what you mean."

He yanked her up then, his face inches from her own, his eyes condemning and full of judgment. "Yes, you do. You know exactly what I mean. You see, I know all about it, Trixie. I know you gave our son away right after he was born."

If Logan hadn't been holding her, she would have fallen to the floor and fainted. She felt the blood rushing away from her head, felt her pulse increasing to a dangerously high level, felt the imprint of his hands on her arms, steadying her, holding her up even as he held her body away.

"You know?" she managed to ask, stunned that he'd kept it a secret all of this time. Stunned with understanding. This, this was why he'd resented her so much! He'd known, dear God, he'd known from the very beginning. And if what he was telling her now was the truth—

"Oh, yeah, I know," Logan said, the confession pouring through him like a rushing river tearing through a dam. "I've known since the day your father brought Caleb to the ranch when he was only a few days old—to his home, to me." Holding her close, his hands gripping her arms, his eyes boring into her, he said, "I know, because, you see, I'm his father. But you already know that, of course. At least that much isn't a lie."

He let her go then, stepping back to run his hands through his hair, his anger at both himself and her boiling down to a slow simmer. Then he looked her in the eyes and told her in a voice quiet with honesty, "But what you didn't know, what I didn't tell you is—you're his mother."

His mother! Images, blurred and hazy, rushed through Trixie's numb mind. This couldn't be true. This had to be some sort of cruel joke.

"No!"

At her gasp of shock, Logan nodded, watching as she gripped the back of the nearest pew for support. "That's right. That's the truth, at last. The little boy lying in that hospital bed is the child you gave up, Trixie. Caleb is your son."

Chapter Twelve

The cruelty of his words struck her with the force of a cold, hard slap.

And then the reality of what he'd just told her set in, causing her whole world to shift off its carefully built foundation.

In that instant all the time she'd spent with Caleb came rushing back, poignant and sweet, flashing through her consciousness like the pages of a photo album. And so did the evasiveness she'd seen in both Logan and Gayle, the distrust she'd sensed from both of them. That image tainted her world, her whole outlook, while it explained so much.

So much. So much time wasted, so many lies told.

Backing away, she shook her head again, her hands covering her mouth. "No, you're lying. That can't be possible. That can't be true."

Logan belatedly realized what he'd just done. He'd let his own rage and guilt color his judgment. Now, seeing the tortured look on her beautiful face, he instantly regretted his actions. He'd never meant to be so blunt, so insensitive.

Reaching for her, he said, "I'm sorry, Trixie. I didn't want to tell you like this, but…well, with everything that's happened…" Groping for the right words now, he finished with a defeated sigh. "I'm so worried, I wasn't thinking straight."

Trixie pushed at him, instinctively trying to get away, then, as the full impact of his words hit her, she came at him with both fists, beating her hands against his chest with all her might. "How could you do this? How could anyone be so cruel, so callous? How? Why?"

Logan stood stoic and still, letting her beat out all of her frustrations and helpless anger on him. He certainly deserved it. And the physical blows didn't hurt half as much as the dejection and hurt in her blue eyes. That was the part he couldn't take.

Funny, he'd always envisioned this very moment, when he would tell her the truth about Caleb. He'd always dreamed of it, thinking he'd feel some small measure of vengeance and triumph. Now, he only felt empty and lost, bitter with himself, guilty for all he'd been a part of, for how he'd made her suffer. And until this very moment, he'd never fully realized just how much she must have suffered. But her misery, her anguish, was there on her face, bruising her, changing her, making her look so vulnerable and afraid. And destroyed.

Now he had to wonder why he'd ever agreed to any of this. Too late. Way too late to start wondering now.

Up until now, he'd laid all the blame at her feet

because he'd believed she didn't care enough to fight for their child, for their love. Well, he'd played a big part in this deliberate charade, and because of that he'd probably lost her forever. Because of that his son might not ever know his real mother.

Logan stood there, seeing Trixie in a new light, seeing the girl who'd become the woman, seeing the innocence of ignorance, blissful ignorance, stripped from her face, along with what little pride she had left.

He wouldn't make her suffer anymore. It was time he told her everything. High time he learned to trust in God and his own faith. He could only hope he hadn't learned too late.

So he stood, holding her while she fought against him, holding her while she cried and sobbed and finally, went completely limp in his arms. Then he pulled her close and hugged her, trying to give comfort where none could be found, trying to find comfort in the arms of the woman he loved.

Finally he lifted her chin with a thumb, and looked into her eyes, for the first time with complete, absolute honesty. "I've wanted to tell you for so long."

Trixie still shook from the shock of it. But through the shock, through the numbing realization, came a little bit of sheer joy. "Caleb is my son," she said on a whispery, breathless voice. "Caleb is my son."

Logan guided her back to one of the pews, then sat down beside her, his arm still around her shoulders. "Yes, he certainly is."

He'd seen that little bit of her in Caleb each and every day of the boy's life. In the blue of his big eyes, in the impish way he tried to get the best of both his father and his grandmother. In the way he'd doted on Brant Dunaway. She was there, had always been there in Caleb's very essence. Each time his son laughed or cried, Logan was reminded of the woman who'd given birth to him, the woman who'd been forced to give him up.

Logan understood that now. Just like him, Trixie had been forced to choose. And it felt good to be able to share this with her at last. At long last.

She got up. "I have to go see him."

"I want you to see him," he said, pushing her back down. "But first, I want you to know everything."

"Why?" she said, her eyes lifting to his. "Why didn't anyone tell me?"

Logan knew the truth was far from being told. There was still more hurt to wade through.

"Well," he began, ripping a hand through his hair, trying to tell her straight, "after you and I...after Brant caught us together, well, you remember how you pleaded with him not to fire me?"

She nodded. She remembered every impassioned word. "I told him I'd never see you again, if he'd just let you keep your job."

"And he did. He never could resist anything you asked of him, and he was a very forgiving person. So it only stands to reason that when you asked him to help you save your baby—"

Trixie hitched another sob. "He did," she said, love for her father pouring through her battered system. "He...he saved my son." Her eyes widened, filled with tears again. "I begged him to. But...he never told me what he did. He never told me."

Logan nodded, then ran a hand over the beard stubble on his face, feeling so drained, so very tired. "But it cost him, Trixie. It cost all of us."

She gripped his arm, a steely determination keeping the anger at bay, keeping the impact of this latest revelation at a distance, until she knew the whole story. "Tell me, Logan. I want to hear all of it."

Logan leaned back against the support of the pew, weary to the bone, his voice raw and raspy. "Pamela called him and told him you were pregnant. She blamed him, of course, for letting you run loose on the ranch, for not watching you, for not watching me. Of course, he didn't tell me any of this until later."

"So you didn't know about the baby right away?"

"No. All I knew was that I loved you and that your father hadn't shot me on sight."

She almost smiled. "He was pretty mad at both of us."

"Yeah, but your mother was even madder, especially at Brant. She made him feel so guilty, especially when she found out he hadn't fired me. She claimed he was putting my welfare above yours." He paused, weighed his next words. "She also accused him of doing it to protect my mother. Or as she termed it, his mistress."

Trixie gasped, stunned. "But that's not true. Your mother told me how things stood between her and my father."

"Yes, but Pamela wanted to think the worst."

Trixie closed her eyes, a terrible scene playing in her mind. How Logan must have hated her when he found out the truth. And Gayle. No wonder the woman had been so hostile toward her. Lowering her head, she said, "I can't believe this."

Logan's next words were rough with emotion. "Brant took her badgering pretty calmly, but when Pamela insisted that you had to give the baby up, he fought for you. He told me all of this later, after...after he'd forgiven both of us, after he'd seen his new grandson. He fought for you, Trixie."

Trixie gazed over at him, wishing she had known, wishing she had had even a glimpse of her baby. Bitterness choked her words. "But mother won, as usual."

"Yeah, I think he had a hard time turning her down, too. He was rough and tough, but he had the softest heart. He went off into the mountains and he didn't come home until he thought it all through. He wanted to do what was right and fair. And, he wanted to protect his daughter."

Logan's words, spoken in such a loving reverence, only added to Trixie's own anguish. She sat silent, remembering bits and pieces of things she'd long ago buried. "So when I called him, begging him to help me, he came, and he had both my mother and me to contend with."

Logan nodded, calmer now, determined to tell her everything. "He was torn. Pamela wanted to hide you away and then get rid of the baby as quickly and quietly as possible."

That hurt. That hurt so very much. But Trixie was used to her mother's misguided shame. It had been her own for so long now. "They never once allowed me to call you or see you, Logan, or to even give you a say in the matter. She told me she'd make it hard for you and your mother. And she would have."

He nodded again, then frowned. "You don't have

to remind me of Pamela's power. She wielded it over Brant and over your grandfather.''

Shocked, Trixie stared at him. ''Granddaddy knows?''

''Everybody knows but you,'' he admitted. When she would have said more, he held up a hand. ''Just let me finish. I need to get this all out of my system.''

She sat back, silent and brooding. All this time she'd felt so guilty, so worthless for her deceit. And all this time, she'd been deceived by the people she'd trusted the most. ''Go on,'' she said in a small voice.

''They argued, a lot. Harlan and Brant wanted to raise the child as a Dunaway. Pamela refused. She threatened, she manipulated, she promised to make life unbearable for everyone involved. Finally Brant told her that he would raise the child here in Arkansas, on the ranch. Once he made up his mind, he was pretty determined, from what he told me later. Pamela knew when to call it quits, but she also saw this as a prime opportunity to get her way.''

Shuddering, Trixie doubled over, the pain of her feelings so physical, it racked her stomach. ''He did it to help me. He wanted to help me.''

''Yes, but Pamela made sure he paid a price for his request. You see, she was concerned about me. She hated me.''

Trixie nodded her understanding. ''No, she wouldn't want you involved, even if she didn't care enough about the baby to raise it herself.''

She refused to think about all of that now. Right now, she only wanted the complete truth, no matter how painful.

And the pain got much, much worse.

Reaching out to take her hand, Logan continued, his words deadly calm, too calm. "They struck up a deal. You would give birth to the baby, then they would take it away. To protect you, they wouldn't allow you to see it or even know if it was a boy or a girl."

The tears flowed down Trixie's face, silent and purging, while she listened and thought about Caleb's beautiful little face and the big blue eyes that looked exactly like Brant Dunaway's. If she hadn't been so preoccupied with the ranch and Logan, she might have seen it earlier. The truth she'd wanted, needed, so badly, had been staring her in the face all along.

Logan's grip on her hand tightened. "Brant agreed to take the child and bring it to the ranch. He would tell me the truth and allow me to be with my child."

Trixie heard the raw pain in his voice, felt the tension in his hand on hers. "And?"

"And in return for that favor, for that privilege, neither Brant nor I could ever have any contact with you again. Even if you tried to see either of us or visit the ranch, we had to turn you away. Oh, and I could never tell you the truth. Never. That was the only way I would be allowed to raise my own child. If I hadn't been so angry and hurt, I would have fought them all, but all I could think about was that you didn't want our baby."

Trixie turned to face him, the blur of tears that clouded her eyes matching the misty regret she saw in Logan's gaze.

"I'm sorry," he said, tears flowing down his face now. "So very sorry." Wanting, needing her to understand, he said, "Do you know how hard that

was—to have to make that choice? But...I never
knew my father. All I knew was that he had abandoned me, left my mother and me. Trixie, I just
couldn't do that to my son. I couldn't. So, I chose
him over you. You weren't the only one who gave
everything up. I had to give you up, so I could have
my son with me.''

"Oh, Logan." She pulled him to her, holding him,
rocking him in her arms. "What other choice did you
have? I know all about the power and persuasion of
the Dunaway dollars. I know you would have done
anything, anything to protect Caleb."

"Except tell his mother," he said, the weight of
his guilt suffocating him. He raised his head, then
brought his hands up to her face. "Do you know how
much I loved you? You can't know how many times
I thought about taking Caleb and running away, to
find you. I wanted to, so bad. Then I remembered that
I was just a field hand and you—you had this wonderful, bright future that didn't include a bum and a
baby. So I went off to college at Brant's insistence,
and I left my baby with him and my mother—I only
saw Caleb on weekdays and holidays. Then I married
Donna, just to ease the pain, just to have someone,
anyone to share my beautiful boy with. And the whole
time I thought about you, and how you'd just given
him up without a fight."

Trixie smoothed his hair off his hot brow. "And I
bet my mother made sure you heard all about me, or
at least her version of my life."

"She kept Brant posted, and because I was so bitter, I assumed you just didn't care, that you had put
all of this behind you, that you never really wanted

the baby. So I let my anger be my shield, and I took it out on Donna. I hated you, so I made her life miserable.''

"So she left you, too. And that's why she doesn't have anything to do with Caleb.''

"Yeah. Donna loved the baby, but she couldn't stick around to be a mother to him. We both—Caleb and me—we were a constant reminder of you.'' He lowered his head, then glanced over at her. "And the whole time, the whole time, I thought you didn't care. Brant tried to tell me, but I wouldn't listen. All of these years, I thought you didn't love our child or me.''

"No,'' Trixie said in defense of herself. "I always wanted our child. Always. All those years ago, I dreamed about being with you and our baby. Then, as time passed, I had to give up on that dream. I thought it could never be possible after what I'd done, and so I let my mother rule my life, because I just didn't care anymore.'' Her voice barely above a whisper, she added, "And she knew. All of this time, my mother knew.''

Logan couldn't bring himself to voice how he felt about Pamela Dunaway. Instead he said, "She'd send money, but she never even asked about Caleb. Not once. I think she considered that her way of paying me off, for my silence. But I never wanted her money. Brant put it in a trust fund for Caleb, though. He said that it was Dunaway money, and it belonged to his grandson.''

Trixie closed her eyes, willing the anger and pain to stay away just a little longer. "All of this time, I thought my daddy didn't love me anymore. I thought he was ashamed of me, the same way my mother was ashamed. But he did love me. He loved me enough to make sure my child, his grandchild had a safe, loving home. He gave me up so he could protect our baby. He kept his promise.''

Reaching her hands up to cover Logan's, she gulped back another sob. "Oh, Logan. Logan, help me, help me. I don't think—"

"I'm here," he said, pulling her into his arms again. "I'm here now, Trixie, and I promise I won't desert you or hide away anymore, like the coward I've been. Caleb is our son, together. No more secrets or lies. And no more placing blame.''

She held tightly to him, his strength, his courage making her feel so much better. Then she lifted her head, "But he's so sick. Logan, he has to pull through.''

Logan stared up at the altar, his expression grim. "I wonder...is God punishing us for all this? Is this His way of showing us we can't play with people's lives?''

She rubbed her hand over his, horrified that he could even think such a thing. "No, no. God wouldn't do that, not to Caleb, anyway. He's so innocent in all of this. We have to believe that, Logan. God wouldn't let him die, not now, not when I've finally found him again.''

Without another word between them, they held hands and turned toward the stained-glass window shining down on them. And together they prayed for their son's life.

"One more chance, Lord," Logan said. "That's all

we ask of you. One more chance to make things right with our son.''

A gentle silence flowed around them, offering comfort, offering honesty, offering hope.

Offering redemption, at last.

The silence didn't last long, however. Pamela showed up bright and early the next morning, decked in jewels and jealousy, determined to get her daughter out of the clutches of what she termed ''these Arkansas heathens.''

Spotting Trixie and Logan as they came out of pediatric intensive care, she swept across the hospital corridor in crisp blue linen, her eyes flashing fire at Logan before she turned a pouting face toward her daughter. ''I've come to take you home.''

Trixie didn't know whether to scream or cry. She'd just spent the past few minutes with her son, watching him, touching him, crooning to him, hoping against hope to make him hear her, see her, know her. That had been her ritual all during the night, standing by her son's bed, along with his father, in the few precious minutes when they were allowed in to see him.

Her son.

Even now, hours after Logan had told her that remarkable truth, after she'd walked into Caleb's room with that new, bursting knowledge and touched a tentative hand to his, she still felt a surge of joy rushing through her system each time she said the words in her head.

Her son.

Her son, who now lay in there, so alone, so deep in a dream world, so at peace even when those around him seemed to be falling completely apart, even when his world was changing with each passing minute. Her son, whom her mother had kept away from her all of these years, a little boy who'd been bartered and used, to gain what Pamela believed to be the best for her daughter.

And now, Pamela was here, without a thought for him, demanding that she come home? Suddenly she knew where her home was, and that she would never leave it, or Caleb, again.

"What kind of mother are you?" Trixie said to Pamela in a deadly level tone, her eyes centered on her mother's shocked face. Logan's hand on her arm steadied her enough to keep her from lashing out even more.

"The kind who cares about her daughter's reputation," Pamela replied evenly as she raked her gaze over Logan with unabashed disdain. "Rad is inconsolable, of course, and everyone is talking. This behavior is scandalous, Tricia Maria, and I won't stand for it any longer."

"Tough, because I'm not going anywhere with *you*," Trixie replied, letting go of Logan to push past Pamela before she did something that would really give people cause to talk.

"Tricia Maria, don't do this!"

She could hear her mother's high heels clicking on the hospital tiles, right behind her. It seemed as if that sound had followed her all of her life, taunting her with guilt and blame, haunting her with regret and reprimand.

Waiting until they were out of earshot of the others, Trixie turned to face Pamela, the look on her face causing her mother to step back. "Mother, I don't think I can discuss any of this with you right now. In fact, I want you to leave."

Her mother took one look at her face and suddenly realized the cause of Trixie's unbridled hostility.

"Oh, oh, you know, don't you?" Pamela said on a small gasp of breath. Lifting her chin, she glared down the corridor at Logan. "Of course, *he* couldn't wait to tell you."

Shaking her head, Trixie said, "He waited over seven years, Mother. He waited from the day Caleb was born until now, when he's lying in there near death. Isn't that enough punishment, even for you?"

Pamela lifted her head, surprise temporarily replacing snobbery. "What do you mean, near death? No one would tell me anything when I arrived at the ranch. They just said the boy had had an accident and you were here."

Amazed at her mother's self-involved existence, she said, "Yes, I'm here. Finally. But I should have been here long ago. I'm here, but now it might be too late. The boy, Caleb—his name is Caleb—hit his head after he crashed a four-wheeler, Mother. The boy, who happens to be your grandson by the way, might die."

The impact of that statement stopped Pamela in her kid leather handmade pumps. "Oh, my. Oh, my," she said as she sank down in the nearest chair. "How awful."

Trixie stared down at her, her tone harsh. "Yes, how awful. Another messy tidbit for you to try and clean up and hide under your self-righteous carpet.

Hurry, Mother, run fast so you won't be caught associating with this group of sinners and losers.''

Appalled, Pamela said, ''Now, there's really no need to be so vulgar, Tricia.''

''Vulgar?'' Trixie hissed the word at her mother. ''Vulgar? I'll tell you what's vulgar! Vulgar is the way you manipulated my father and Logan into doing this. Vulgar is the way you cajoled my grandfather into going along with this scheme of yours. Vulgar is the way you used a child, *my* child, Mother, to get your own way. When are you going to stop playing with people's lives? When?''

Pamela didn't speak. Instead, she just sat looking up at her daughter. Finally, with a long-suffering sigh, she said, ''I only did what I thought was best. And I'm truly sorry that the child is hurt. But, think, Tricia, think. You can't possibly tell that boy who you really are. Not now.'' Her shrug was as indifferent as it was elegant. ''Why, it's way too late now. You would only make things worse for him, and for yourself, too, of course.''

Without taking a breath, without stopping to see the pain her words were inflicting on her daughter, Pamela rushed on, ''No, let's just leave things the way they are. I'll take care of all his hospital expenses, of course. He'll have the best of care. But you, you need to come on back home to Dallas, darling, and patch things up with Rad—I've already smoothed the way there for you. He loves you, so he's willing to forgive and forget. Then you can put all of this behind you for good. It's really for the best.''

Trixie gasped in horror as she realized that once

again, her mother was trying to manipulate her life. Once again, Pamela was willing to pay any price to keep all of this a secret. And she was also willing to pull out all the stops to keep her daughter away from Logan and the baby Trixie had given up so long ago. Oh, she knew exactly which buttons to push. Only this time she'd pushed too far.

But she was right. How could Trixie just march into Caleb's room and announce, "Oh, glad you're all right and by the way, I'm your mother."

The brief period of joy Trixie had felt at finding out the truth was gone now, replaced by the cold, ugly glare of her mother's spiteful, pointed observations. How would she ever be able to face her son? How could a mother tell a child that she'd let him go and now she was back to make up for all the lost time, all the lost dreams?

The anger, the shock, the delayed reaction to everything that had happened in the past few days and hours, hit Trixie squarely in the face as she stood there looking down at her mother's beautiful, deceitful, hypocritical face, every nerve in her body going into overload.

"Was it best," she began, spitting the words at Pamela, her hands shaking, her mind raging, "to take a child from its mother? Was it best to make Logan and my own father choose between that child and me? Was it best to have everyone involved in the situation lie, including me? How can you actually sit there and say that to me with a straight face, Mother? How can you spout out platitudes about Christian values, when you've never applied those values to your own life? How?"

Pamela stopped pretending then. Frightened, she stood to try and touch her daughter, to offer comfort. But Trixie was beyond comfort. With a growl she shook Pamela's hand away. "If Caleb dies, I will never forgive you."

With that she headed out the door, out of the hospital, away from the pain and the agony of all that she had lost, of all the minutes and hours of tiny pleasures she'd been denied with her son. She longed to go to him, to shake him awake, to make him see that she loved him so very dearly. But in her heart she felt she didn't deserve to be here. She didn't deserve his love, and she certainly didn't deserve Logan's love. No wonder he'd hated her all of these years. It was no more than she hated herself right now.

And, for his sake, for her son's sake, she would probably never be able to tell Caleb that she was his mother. If he even lived to see her face again.

She headed out the lobby, mindless of Logan calling to her.

"Trixie, wait. Wait, please. Trixie, come back. Caleb needs you. I need you."

Meeting Harlan on the steps, she said, "Give me the car keys."

Her grandfather looked her over and shook his head. "No. You're in no condition to drive."

Angry at him too, she retorted, "And you're in no position to stop me."

Hurt, Harlan reluctantly handed her the keys. "I'm sorry, child," he said as he watched her hurry away.

Trixie turned back, respect for her grandfather overriding her own frustration. Running back to grab him by the arm, she said, "I don't blame you. I blame myself. I should have fought harder. I should have come back here to Logan."

"I know that now," Harlan said, his eyes watering up. "I wasn't thinking straight back then. I was only worried about the Dunaway name. I forgot to worry about the Dunaway family. I should have stood by you."

"I understand," Trixie said. "And…I just want to go to my father's grave, just for a little while. I have some…some things to say to him."

Harlan let her go then, with a loving pat on the arm. "Okay, but be careful. And, Trixie, remember that he loved you above all else."

"I know that now," she replied as she walked away. "Granddaddy," she said over her shoulder, her voice hitching, "stay with him, please. Stay with Caleb until I can…until I can face him again."

"I will," Harlan replied. "But…you come on back when you're feeling better about things, okay?"

Trixie didn't answer him. She wasn't sure if she'd ever feel better about things.

Logan, however, wasn't going to let her get away so easily this time. "Trixie, wait," he said as he headed her off at Harlan's car. "Don't leave."

She lifted her gaze to his, saw the pain of her soul mirrored in his troubled eyes. "I have to…I have to think about all of this. I…I don't think I should be here when he wakes up. I don't want to confuse him."

Logan touched a hand to her face. "You won't. He needs you. You're his mother. Right now that's all that matters. We'll work out the details later."

She looked down at the door handle. "But he doesn't know that—he doesn't know me. How can we ever tell him that?"

"We'll work it out somehow," Logan said, his rough hand soft on her skin. "Will you come back inside?"

She shook her head, then looked down. "I can't. I'm so ashamed."

Pulling her close, Logan said, "We all played a part in this, honey. And I won't let you go off alone in this shape." Anger coloring his next statement, he added, "And I won't let your mother do this to you, to us, again. Don't listen to her, Trixie."

Running a hand through her hair, Trixie whispered, "I just need some time alone. I can't be in the same room with my mother right now." Then, "Logan, I want to go see my father. I need to talk to him, I need to be near him right now."

Understanding dawning in his eyes, Logan nodded, then backed away. "Okay. Fine. You need to be near Brant? Then come on back and stay by your son's side. That's where a part of your father will always be. I mean it, Trixie. I won't let you go this time."

She had to know. "Even if Caleb dies?"

Logan's face turned ashen. "He won't. Remember, God didn't bring us this far without a reason. I'm counting on that to save my son's life. And I'm counting on you, to stay here this time. Don't run away again."

Trixie watched as he reached out a hand to her.

She didn't want to leave Caleb. But after the sickening conversation with her mother, she felt dirty and disillusioned. Caleb had Logan to watch over him.

He'd always had his father. Always. And thankfully he'd had his grandfather for a few years at least.

But he might not ever have his mother. And the fact that he might not even have her in the last hours of his young life only added to her agony. He might die, never knowing, never seeing, how much she loved him.

Unless she was there by his side, regardless of the outcome. Gulping back fresh tears, she took Logan's hand. She couldn't leave Caleb. Even with her mother's cruel words ringing inside her head, she still couldn't leave her little boy.

Logan let out a relieved breath, then guided her across the parking lot. Without a word, they went back inside the hospital to stand by their son's bed.

"Mommy's sorry, baby," Trixie said, tears flowing down her face as she rubbed his little arm. "Mommy's so sorry. But I promise, I'm going to be right here with you from now on."

This time she would follow her heart.

Chapter Thirteen

Logan watched Trixie as she sat by Caleb's side, memories of all that happened to them racing through his weary mind. Things might have turned out so differently back then, if he'd known she was carrying his child. For one thing, he would never have let her get away. But they had both been too young and afraid to take matters into their own hands.

This time, he promised himself, *this time I won't let her go.* This time it would be different.

But before that could happen, Caleb had to get well.

Feeling completely helpless, Logan walked out into the quiet hospital corridor. He might not be able to hold on to Trixie just yet, and he alone certainly didn't have the power to bring his child back, but there was one thing he could do right now that would make him feel a whole lot better. Logan needed to have a long-overdue talk with Mrs. Pamela Dunaway.

He found Pamela sitting in the same spot where

Trixie had left her, mainly because Harlan had ordered her to stay there. Logan came into the waiting area near pediatrics to find Harlan standing over a pouting Pamela like a raging bull about to charge.

"You aren't going to bully her—not this time," Harlan said. "You've badgered that child all of her life, trying to turn her into a replica of yourself. And I've stood by and watched you, only because I thought you had her best interest at heart." He paused, swallowed. "But the things Gayle told me you said to Trixie here today, the way you made her ashamed to face her own child—that was just downright underhanded, Pamela. I can see now what I should have seen long ago. You don't care about your daughter's happiness. Your only interest is in protecting yourself. Apparently you only care about something when you can gain from it."

Pointing his forefinger at his daughter-in-law, he told her, "All of these years I allowed you to stay a part of this family, because I believe in family and because I thought it was in Trixie's best interest to have her mother around. But not anymore. Not anymore.

"She's a grown woman now, and she has a good head on her shoulders, and a fine, big old heart just like her daddy's. I won't let you ruin her chance to find some peace and happiness with her son and Logan, the way you ruined your own chance with Brant. Do I make myself clear?"

Pamela's round eyes widened in utter surprise. "Perfectly," she said, her legs crossed primly, one foot swinging in an angry arc of anxiety. Harlan might be an old softy, but he still wielded the power that paid her bills. She knew when to tread softly with him. Beseeching him now, she said, "So, what am I supposed to do? Just sit here and watch her throw her life away?"

Logan had had enough at this point. Stalking toward Pamela, he said, "What makes you so all-knowing? What makes you the one who gets to call the shots in Trixie's life?"

Giving him a look of total disdain, Pamela continued to swing her foot. "I'm her mother. Isn't that reason enough to stop her from making a tragic mistake?"

Logan scoffed, then stared down at her. "No, being her mother doesn't give you the right to control her life, even if you believe she may be heading down the wrong road. But that's what you've done ever since you lost Brant. You used your daughter to punish him, and then you used your own flesh and blood—your own grandson, to control all of us."

Mad now, Pamela rose off her chair with all the grace of a queen, then waved a hand in dismissal. "Somebody had to be rational. Brant always was too sentimental and emotional. I had to be the calm one. I had to be the one who always played the heavy. I'm sorry if that offends you, Mr. Maxwell."

Logan stepped closer, his eyes flashing darkly. "What offends me, Mrs. Dunaway, is the fact that you think you're above reproach, that you think you're such a perfect Christian that none of the rest of us can possibly keep up with you or even aspire to ask your forgiveness."

Pamela hissed, "What you did to my daughter was unforgivable."

"I agree," he said, nodding, "but if you had been willing, Trixie and I could have made a decision to do right by our child. Sure, we got carried away, we made a mistake in judgment, but we were both willing to own up to that mistake. Only, you refused to let that happen. You didn't even let us decide what to do about our own child."

She glared at him, disgust evident in her words. "No, because I always expected my daughter to do better than the likes of you. I couldn't allow her to marry so young and to a man she barely knew."

Logan threw his hands up, then dropped them at his side. "I was good enough for Brant. I was good enough to raise my son. And I'm good enough for Trixie. You see, she loves me. So, frankly, your opinion of me means very little to me at this point. But for Trixie's sake, I do wish you'd try to step out of that narrow-minded notion of yours."

Pamela lifted her shoulders, then turned away. "My notions are based on my values and my beliefs."

Pulling her back around, Logan replied, "Then, lady, you have a really skewed idea of what the word of Jesus Christ is all about. You just don't get it, do you?"

Lifting her chin to a haughty level, she said, "No, Mr. Maxwell, I guess I don't. Why don't you set me straight on something I've been taught all my life, since you seem to know so much more about my own religion than I possibly could."

Thoroughly fed up, Logan took her by the arm. Lifting her up off the chair she'd been perched on, he practically dragged her down the hospital hallway.

"All right, you want to know what I'm trying to tell you? Then, follow me. I'll show you the real meaning of the love of Jesus Christ."

Harlan let them pass, his eyes full of admiration and apprehension for Logan. Let the boy have his turn. He'd certainly waited long enough, and now his son was near death. It was high time they all accepted their fate and learned to love again. He just prayed it wasn't too late.

Gayle, too, just sat there, watching, wondering, hoping that maybe Logan could talk some sense into that high-handed, overblown socialite. Then she prayed for both of them.

But most of all she prayed for her grandson.

"Let go of me!" Pamela demanded, furious at being manhandled by this field hand in a public place. Glancing around to make sure none of the busy nurses had seen anything, she hissed, "Where are you taking me?"

Logan stared straight ahead, his hand on her arm light but firm. "To see your grandson—and your daughter," he replied over his shoulder, the dare in his voice too real to miss.

"No." Pamela tried to pull back at the doors of the pediatric intensive care unit, a horrified look marring her wrinkle-free face. "I...I don't think this is wise."

Logan whirled to give her a harsh stare. "Why? Because 'out of sight, out of mind' is the way you want to keep him? Or maybe because he'll remind you of Brant too much, and that might actually make you feel just a pinch of guilt?" Tugging her through the doors, he dared any of the nurses to try and stop him. In a low whisper, he continued, "Or maybe, just maybe, you'll recognize Trixie in that little boy in there, and that might be too much for even your hardened soul to bear."

Trying to pull back, Pamela said, "Don't make me do this. I won't go in there."

Logan refused to let her go. But...there was real fear in her eyes. That surprised him; he'd always pictured Trixie's mama as such a formidable, fearless person. Perhaps there was a soft spot somewhere behind that haughty demeanor, after all.

More gently he said, "You need to see your grandson. He might not make it, unless we all pull together and show him we love him." Leaning close, he added, "And please, think about Trixie for once. She just found out she's his mother. She needs your support right now, not your criticism."

Pamela's alabaster skin turned even more pale as she stood there, frozen. Finally she looked up and glanced around, her eyes full of sincere appeal. "You don't understand. I...I can't tolerate hospitals. Ever since Brant—"

Logan saw it all so clearly now. "Ever since Brant got hurt in the rodeo?"

She nodded, a brisk bobbing of her head, then closed her eyes tightly shut. "All the blood, all the stitches. I thought...I thought he was going to die. I begged him to give it up, but he loved the rodeo more than he loved me."

Feeling a strong sympathy for her in spite of all she'd done, Logan said, "You're wrong there. He loved you more than anything. He loved you till the day he died.''

''How do you know that?'' she asked, her eyes bright with stubborn tears as she looked directly at him for the first time.

''He told me,'' Logan said, his voice calm and sure. ''He told me to tell Trixie he loved her, then he told me to take good care of his grandson.'' His hand tender on her arm now, he added, ''And the last thing he said was, 'And Pammy. You know, son, I sure do love my Pammy. Wish I could see her pretty face one more time.' And then, he died.''

The tears came then, falling down her face in soft rivulets. And with the tears, her heart opened just a little, like a shy flower. ''But…he left me. I gave him an ultimatum and he…he chose the ranch and the rodeo over me.''

''No,'' Logan said in a whisper, ''you drove him away by demanding perfection, by trying to make him into something he could never be. You see, Brant loved you just the way you were, flaws and all. But you refused to meet him halfway. So the rodeo and his ranch were the only things he had left, except Trixie. And then, you even managed to take her away from him.''

Logan's voice, usually so deep and firm, cracked with the weight of a broken heart. Pointing to the room where Caleb lay a few feet away, he said, ''That little boy in there was Brant's only consolation. And Brant loved him—he gave all the love he still had for you and Trixie to his grandson. And now, all I'm asking of you, all I want from you, is a little consideration for that love. Let go of the grudge, let go and let God take over. Open your heart, Mrs. Dunaway, and help me to save my son—your grandson.'' Giving her a gentle nudge, he added, ''Or do you want to risk losing Trixie, too?''

Pamela actually looked humble, and more than a little ashamed. She stood there, so silent, so unmoving, her expression changing from stubborn and resentful to understanding and hopeful. Glancing up at Logan, she said, ''But…he's so tiny, so young. And he doesn't even know me.''

Logan heard the hidden message in her plea. She didn't want to get too attached to someone she might lose. He could sure understand that feeling. He'd protected Caleb all this time for that very reason. He'd worried about losing his son to Trixie, to her way of life. Selfishly, he'd been glad that Caleb didn't know his mother. And now he realized, too late, none of that was important.

Brant had died without being able to tell Caleb that he was his own flesh and blood. Now Caleb might die, never knowing how very much he was loved, never knowing he had a mother who'd sacrificed so much because she loved him.

He turned back to Pamela now, hoping to make her see what he'd been too blind to see. ''It doesn't matter. He'll know you're there. A few precious moments of happiness are a lot more important than holding a grudge and blaming everyone for one mistake. My son was not a mistake. He was a beautiful gift, and I'm just thankful that God saw fit for me to be a part of his life. And if he makes it, he can get to know you, and you and Trixie can finally be in his life, too.''

Pamela still looked skeptical and confused. "Won't that only make things worse?"

Hearing the catch of doubt in her question, Logan pushed on. "How can loving a child make that child's life worse? Love heals all wounds, Mrs. Dunaway. Love brings joy and pleasure and hope. Haven't we all paid the price of sin and sorrow? Isn't it time…isn't it time to put all of that behind us and do what's right for Caleb?"

She looked up at him then, her eyes devoid of any hostility. "And Trixie," she said, her tone gentle and meek, awe filled. "I need to do right by my daughter, don't I?"

"That's the idea," Logan said, relief washing over him. He knew in his heart that Trixie wouldn't be able to love her own child until she felt worthy in her mother's eyes. Oh, she loved Caleb. That came without saying. But she didn't think she deserved to be near him.

But Caleb deserved all of the love this family could offer him.

Starting now.

"Come on," he said. "Just hold his hand. Help Trixie and me to bring him back."

Pamela stepped forward, then dried her eyes, a new look of determination dawning across her face. "All right. I'll try."

Logan guided her into the room, his gaze falling across his son's face before sweeping over all the tubes and machines that were keeping Caleb alive. His eyes meeting Trixie's, he whispered, "I brought someone with me."

Trixie looked up, her red-rimmed eyes going wide

at the sight of her mother standing there. Her first instinct was to tell Pamela to get out, but something in the gentle, confused expression of her mother's face stopped her.

"Oh," Pamela said, her hand flying to her mouth as she gazed down on Caleb's peaceful face. "Oh, the poor baby."

Logan took one of Caleb's little hands, rubbing it tenderly, a smile holding his own tears at bay. "Hey, sport, you've got a special visitor. This is—" He looked over at Pamela for support.

Taking Caleb's other hand, she tentatively stepped closer to the bed, her gaze touching on Trixie's face before she looked down at Caleb. "Hello," she said, her voice hitching. "I'm…I'm your…I'm your other grandmother. And I sure hope you wake up so we can get acquainted." She was silent for a minute, then with a bright smile, she said, "You know, I would just love to spoil you rotten. Why, I'll take you to Disney World and the giant water park all the kids love so much." She dashed the tears off her face with one bejeweled hand. "I'll buy you the moon, if you'll only wake up."

Logan didn't say anything. He couldn't speak. He looked over at Trixie's amazed expression, his gaze reassuring. He'd worry about Pamela Dunaway spoiling his son later. Right now, he had to agree with her. Right now, the lump in his throat was about to burst wide open. One prayer answered, he thought as he watched Pamela's expression change from tentative and unsure to determined and uncondemning.

Logan felt as if he and Trixie had just witnessed a miracle. As she held her grandson's hand for the first time, Pamela's expression changed from harsh and unyielding to soft and maternal, all in the space of a few precious minutes. She was a beautiful woman, always had been. But what he saw there in her eyes now was an inner beauty that came from a certain peace, and a certain acceptance. Pamela Dunaway still had the fight left in her, only now she would fight for Caleb and for Trixie.

"He looks so much like Brant," she said, a gasp of awe sighing through her words. Then looking over at her daughter, she added, "And you, darling. He looks a lot like you. He's a beautiful little boy."

Trixie couldn't speak. Instead, she reached across the bed to take her mother's outstretched hand.

"Yes, he is," Logan agreed. "And he needs his mother."

Pamela looked over at Logan then. "Do you love my daughter, Mr. Maxwell?"

Logan returned her intense stare. "Always have."

"Does she love you?"

"I believe so."

Trixie spoke then, her words husky and thick. "Yes, I do love him, Mother. And, I love my son, too."

Pamela stood silent for a while, her fingers tracing a line over Caleb's limp wrist, her beautiful ageless face changing, shifting with each warring thought. Finally, she said, "Then I think you'd better grab hold of that love, while you still have a chance."

Coming around the bed to hug Trixie close, she started to cry. "I'm so sorry, honey. I was wrong. You should be with your child...and with the man you love."

"Do you mean that?" Trixie asked. "Will you stop interfering and let us just be happy together?"

"I'll do my best," Pamela said honestly. "It won't be easy. I'm very set in my ways, and I'm very used to getting my way."

Logan shot Trixie a reluctant grin. At least she was being straight with them. "We'll help you," he said, his eyes touching on hers with a new respect.

"All right then," Pamela replied, her old spunk returning. "That's settled. You two need to find a quiet corner and talk—get something to eat."

Trixie shook her head. "But—"

"No buts. I'll stay here with…with Caleb. And your mother and Harlan are still here. We'll watch over him."

"No fighting?" Logan asked, already reaching for Trixie.

Pamela scoffed. "Mr. Maxwell, I don't cause scenes in public." Then she smiled wryly. "No more fighting. I promise." She looked up at him, her gaze completely serious. "We'll be much too busy praying."

Logan nodded, then taking a shocked Trixie by the hand, tiptoed toward the door.

"Oh, and one other thing," Pamela called in a hushed voice. She gave Trixie a meaningful look. "After you've rested a bit, I'd like to talk to you."

"All right, Mother," Trixie said, still awestruck by her mother's amazing attitude change. "I'll be here."

"So will I, darling. So will I."

Trixie stood on a small open terrace overlooking the busy hospital parking lot below, watching as the evening sun shifted lazily behind the mountain range to the west. The distant vista was colored in muted hues of gold, green and red, glistening and glinting with a warm autumn fire that took her breath away.

In that brilliant autumn beauty, she found some of her strength again. *Please, God, take care of my son. Let him find the sun again. Let him live.*

She'd cried. Oh, how she'd cried. Sitting by her son's bed, she had, as Logan had suggested, found a part of her father. So she'd poured out her heart to him at last.

"I love you, Daddy. And I want to thank you for taking such good care of my son. He's so like you— it's only right that you turned out to be the one to help raise him."

Maybe God had formed a plan for all of them, she thought now as she listened to the bees humming around the carefully-tended hospital flower beds and heard squirrels frolicking in a nearby oak. Off in the distance, the loblolly pines swayed in the crisp fall breeze, soothing her soul with a lullaby sent straight from the heavens.

Maybe God had known that Caleb would grow and thrive right here where he'd been conceived. Maybe Logan had been the right one to raise their child. Caleb had been safe here in Arkansas's gentle hills, nurtured, loved, protected much in the same way as Brant's beloved sunflowers. Knowing that he had been in a safe and loving environment gave her some comfort. Yet she'd missed out on so much of his life. So much.

She looked past the clutter of buildings, to the valley leading out to the hills, watching as a few early golden and orange-colored oak leaves let go and fell gracefully to the earth, and she dreamed a beautiful dream.

In her mind, there stood the house Logan had described to her, all whitewashed and country fresh, with geraniums growing in large pots by the open front door. And in the yard Caleb rode a spirited pony while Logan instructed and encouraged and taught his son the cowboy way. She stood on the porch watching and laughing; loving the two most important men in her life.

And off in the distance, high on a mountain that reached almost to the clouds, she could imagine her father sitting astride a big roan, his hat dipped low over his brow, his laughing blue eyes bright and clear as he called out to his grandson. "Go, little cowboy. Ride that horse. Get back up now. Gotta try again, son. We're all rooting for you, Caleb."

The tears came again. Blinking, she wondered if she'd imagined the scene; it seemed so very real. But the valley was far away in the distance, and the only sounds she heard were those of the traffic, followed by the rustle of falling leaves blowing across the asphalt parking lot below. The sky was rich with the promise of another brilliant sunset.

Would she ever stop crying?

Earlier, she'd gone to the little hospital chapel again and prayed there amid the pine benches and paneled walls, there in the cool darkness of a peaceful, quiet sanctuary. At last, a sanctuary.

Please, Lord, forgive me for what I did. Forgive me for giving my child away, for letting them take my child from me. Did I have a choice? I didn't think so.

But now she did have a choice. Now she'd been given this wonderful, miraculous second chance.

And she was scared to death.

What if Caleb died?

What if he lived, yet didn't want anything to do with her?

What if she could never, ever tell him the truth?

There were other problems to consider, too. Would Logan be willing to share their son with her? He'd had Caleb to himself for so long. Would he be willing to let her take over some of the responsibility?

None of that mattered now, she told herself as she sat there on the terrace, waiting for Logan to bring their dinner.

Just let him live.

That's all she asked now. She'd figure out the rest as it came along. And with God's help, she'd find a way.

Just let him live, Lord.

Did the angels hear her?

She looked up then at the sound of boots clicking on the stone walkway. Looked up and saw Logan coming toward her, his dark eyes rich with unspoken promises, his expression as sure and grounded as the mountains, his hat shading his face so she couldn't really tell what he was thinking.

Trixie got up, her heart pumped with a mixture of pride and longing. She couldn't bear it if—

"Logan?" She rushed to meet him, reaching out a hand to touch his arm. "Logan?"

Logan dropped the sandwiches he'd picked up in the hospital cafeteria, then held her tight against him.

"Don't look so worried, baby. Your mama knows where we are. If anything happens, she'll send word."

Trixie fell against him, savoring the warmth, the strength he offered, a great relief washing through her. "I still can't believe my mother's actually—"

Logan lifted her away, then cupped her face with his hands. "Listen to me, Tricia Maria. This is real. Your mother saw the love in that room—that's what changed her."

"That has to be it," Trixie agreed. "It's like a miracle. She changed, right there before my eyes. She took one look at our child and…her heart opened."

"Love does that," Logan said, his own eyes watering up in spite of his best efforts to hold back. "I always wanted your family to…to just accept me. And now, because of Caleb, your mother's done just that."

Trixie saw the pride in his eyes, but she also saw the pain he'd suffered for so long. Softly, gently, with all the love in her heart, she pulled his head down on her shoulder, cradling him as he cried. How long had he held these tears? How long had he played the part of the tough cowboy, always out mending fences when he'd desperately needed someone to help him mend his own broken heart?

Determined now, Trixie held him close. "Logan, I love you. I love you so much."

He could only nod, but she knew he loved her, too. He'd loved her enough to raise their son; he'd loved her enough to confront her mother. He'd loved her enough to wait for her all these years.

She tugged his head up, then wiped his tears away with her fingers. "And I tell you this, I refuse to let our son die. You're right. This isn't about me or how sorrowful I feel. I don't have time to feel sorry for myself. And it isn't about whether Caleb will accept me or not. Right now I just want to be with my son, even if...even if it's only for a little while." She smiled through her tears. "It's all so simple, really. I've been searching for answers, when the answer is right here, in my heart. I've been handed a second chance, with you and Caleb."

Logan touched a hand to her face. "I love you."

He kissed her then, his touch as soft as the sun's glow to the west, as full of warmth and promise as the rich mountains off in the distance.

With that kiss, with his firm declaration, Trixie found the strength she needed to face her son. "I love you, and...I will make Caleb see that I love him, too. Somehow."

Logan flapped his hat against his jeans, then wiped a determined hand across his wet face. Giving her another quick kiss for luck, he said, "Well, let's hurry up and eat, so we can go back and tell him."

For the first time since she'd learned that Caleb was her son, Trixie felt a certain peace. They'd get through this, with a little help from above. Hopeful, she looked off toward the west, envisioning the spot of earth where her father lay buried. Envisioning the sunflowers.

Chapter Fourteen

⟨decorative flourish⟩

Trixie walked back into the hospital, a new determination coursing through her blood. She would not leave her son again. Ever.

Pamela was there, watching over Caleb, quiet and serene, the same determination her daughter possessed pushing her beyond herself as she harassed the doctors and made sure the nurses weren't neglecting her grandson. She took turns with Gayle and Harlan, each of them cooing to Caleb, talking to him, singing sweet songs to him, telling him to come back, to wake up and make mischief. Each of them telling him to live, that he was loved. Each of them praying, hoping, that he'd wake up.

Trixie stood now, tired, but unyielding, unwilling to surrender the son she'd just discovered to death.

"You are so precious," she whispered as she stroked Caleb's head just underneath the bandage protecting his wounds. "And I called Samantha and had her bring you something. I know you think you have to earn this, but I've decided to go ahead and give it to you.''

She placed the small open box on the bed by Caleb's still little hand. ''It's the Ring of Honor that your…that Brant promised you. You are a true all-around cowboy, and you deserve this.''

She looked down at the glittering ring, wishing with all of her heart that it would provide the healing power needed to wake her son up. The big ring sparkled and winked, its diamonds like beacons as she lifted it high to show Caleb this coveted treasure. ''It's yours, all yours.''

Her son remained asleep.

Trixie tried again. ''Look, I brought your cowboy hat, too. You can wear it again, once that sore spot on your head gets better. Caleb, can you hear me? You need to wake up and put this hat on.''

He looked so peaceful, so perfect. Where was he in his dreamland? Was he out riding the range with Brant, roping stray steers? Was he sitting at the Astrodome, watching his favorite baseball player hit a home run? Was he down at the pond reeling in a big, fat bass, or high up in the mountains watching her from above? Could he hear her voice, see the love she wanted him to find?

''Caleb,'' she said, her hands touching here and there on his still body. ''Caleb. Mommy loves you so much. I know I let you go, so long ago. I didn't want to. I wanted to keep you near. I wanted to hold you and rock you and smell your sweet baby smell while I kissed the top of your head. I missed out on all of that, but I'm here now. And I won't leave you again. Can you hear me, Caleb? Do you know how much I love you and your daddy? Please, baby, please let me have a second chance.''

Logan stood at the door, his own heart shattering in two as he watched Trixie trying desperately to bring their son back to them. If he'd had any doubts about her, or his love for her, those doubts were now gone.

He loved her. Completely. Unconditionally.

And he wondered why he'd blamed her for so long. Why had he let his pride hold him back, hold his son back, from her? Brant had tried to tell him, but he hadn't been willing to listen. He wanted to believe the worst about Trixie.

So much wasted time, so much bitterness. Now none of it seemed so important. Now he only wanted her and their son to be with him.

Stepping into the room, he touched Trixie on the arm. She looked tired and forlorn, worn. Her hair hung limply around her face and dark circles marred her usually bright blue eyes. "Come on," he said. "You need a break."

She held tight to Caleb's hand. "I don't want to leave him."

"Your mother will take over. Just for a few minutes. I have something I want to give you."

Her eyes widening, she looked up at him. "Sounds intriguing, but I'm not interested. Especially if it's another cup of hospital coffee."

"I think you'll appreciate it," he said, the warmth of his words assuring her that this surprise would be a good one. "We'll be just outside, I promise."

Pamela came in then, looking about as frazzled as Trixie had ever seen her. She'd pulled her sleek hair back in a prim ponytail at the nape of her neck, and in spite of being wrinkled, her clothes still hung in graceful lines around her slender body. Her face was haggard, most of the carefully applied makeup now faded and streaked.

Trixie never remembered her mother looking more beautiful.

"Go with Logan, dear," Pamela said, her smile gentle. "I'll stay with him for a while."

"Okay." Still amazed at her mother's change of heart, Trixie squeezed Pamela's hand, then turned and gave her son a kiss. "I'll be right outside and I'll be back soon, sport."

She watched as Pamela picked up Brant's ring box. "I remember this."

"He promised it to Caleb," Trixie explained, hoping Pamela wouldn't argue about it.

Pamela laughed, then looked down at Caleb. "He'll have to do some growing to fit it on his finger."

She glanced back up at her daughter then. Their eyes met in a silent promise and a guaranteed truce. Mother and daughter, fighting on the same side, instead of against each other, at last.

"Go on, honey," Pamela said. "When you get back, we'll...we'll have a nice talk."

Trixie nodded. "Thank you, Mother."

Pamela shot her a surprised smile. It had been a long time since she'd heard those words from her daughter's lips.

Once they were outside the pediatric ICU, Logan took Trixie to a quiet corner of the deserted waiting area. It was near midnight and most visitors had gone home long before.

"Mama and Harlan went down to the cafeteria for a few minutes," he explained.

Wary, Trixie gave him a worried look. "Why all the mystery? Is there something the doctors haven't told me?"

"No, no," Logan said, reassuring her with a quick hug. "I just wanted to show you this…and I thought you might like some privacy while you look it over."

He handed her a large album. "It's Caleb's baby book, complete with pictures from the day he was brought home till now. You missed out on all of that, but Brant…well, he was a stickler for keeping scrap-books."

Trixie bobbed her head, her heart racing. "Daddy had tons of scrapbooks—all his awards, from 4-H and Cub Scouts, to the rodeo. He and mother made me keep one, too."

"Well, he did the same thing for his grandson," Logan said, his voice hushed. "And I want you to have this."

Touched beyond words, Trixie took the thick, leather-covered book in her arms, hugging it close to try and absorb the essence of her son. "Thank you, Logan," she said, her voice hitching. "I thought I'd cried all my tears, but this—"

She couldn't finish. Logan hugged her again, then whispered, "Take your time. You look it over, then if you have any questions, I'll be glad to tell you all the stories about your son. I won't leave anything out."

Trixie took the book in her lap. For a few minutes

she just sat there, running her hands over the smooth burgundy leather. Caleb's initials were etched in its center, in gold. C. L. M.

Caleb Logan Maxwell.

Her child.

Carefully she opened the book, restraining herself from tearing through the many pages. She was so hungry for a glance into her son's life, but she also wanted to savor each and every minute of this precious gift.

And she did. Time seemed to flow into one smooth, complete line as Trixie stared down at the beautiful baby in the pictures before her. Caleb, sleeping in baby blue, in a small crib. Caleb, smiling at the camera, sitting up, his first tooth front and center. Caleb, crawling across the kitchen floor, his chubby little knees smudged with dust and dirt.

Her son. Taking his first steps, with Logan grinning in the background.

Her father, holding Caleb on his knee, Brant's leg bouncing as Caleb rode the imaginary pony and laughed. Brant and Caleb, both in cowboy hats, at Christmas, opening presents underneath a majestic, brightly decorated cedar tree.

Logan with Caleb, up on Rocky, looking like partners in crime. Only, she knew these two were the good guys. Grinning. Playing. Loving.

So many pictures. So many moments snapped and held, cherished. Fishing trips. Campouts. Cub Scouts. Football. Baseball. Bike riding. Horse riding. Swimming in the pond. Worms. Crickets. Frogs. Bugs. Muddy tennis shoes, dirty cowboy boots. Dirt-streaked faces. Grins and smiles. Laughter. Tears.

And finally, Caleb standing in the sunflower patch, holding on to a fat, yellow blossom that stood as tall as him. A little boy doing all the things little boys did.

Her child. Her little boy.

The same little boy who now lay so still, so quiet in a hospital room, with tubes and machines keeping him alive.

She reached the end of the book, and flipped it over, only to start all over again, memorizing each moment, imagining in her mind what it would have been like to be there with him. She read and reread the pictures, adding her own version of each scene, playing out Caleb's young life over and over in her mind, until she knew in her heart that she would never be able to get enough of this, of him.

"He can't die," she said to the empty hallway. Night wore on, dawn was coming. Trixie waited for the sunrise, and the hope of a new day. "He can't die."

Pamela came out to sit by her, silently taking her hand, holding Trixie's fingers interlaced through her own.

"We won't let him die," she told her daughter.

For a minute Trixie believed her. After all, Pamela Dunaway always got her way. For a moment Trixie wanted to hate her mother all over again, but the fight was gone now. The only fight she had left was for Caleb.

"Why, mother?" she asked, her voice raw and raspy. "Why did we send him away?"

Pamela clasped her daughter's hand tightly in her own. "I've asked myself that question a lot over the

last few hours. And believe it or not, I've often wondered that very same thing over the years
since…since all of this happened. I can only tell you
that I was afraid.''

Trixie understood that emotion, but she needed
more. ''Afraid of what?''

Pamela looked at her daughter, then reached up a
hand to stroke Trixie's hair away from her temple.
''Afraid that my friends would talk, afraid I'd lose
my standing within the community, afraid of things
that seem so silly, so trivial now. But mostly, I think,
I was afraid of losing you to your father. You see, I
would have been left with nothing then.''

Trixie saw the desolation in her mother's beautiful
eyes. ''I'd never desert you, Mother.''

Pamela lifted her shoulders in an elegant shrug.
''Your father did, or so I thought. I was bitter and
lonely, and I wasn't so sure about your loyalty, so I
fought for you the only way I knew how. I wasn't
sure about anything, except my need to protect you
and myself.''

''We were selfish,'' Trixie said. ''I was afraid, too.
I was afraid to fight for my own child.''

Pamela's arm tightened around her shoulder. ''No,
you were young, darling. And confused. We did what
we thought was right.''

Trixie stared over at her, desperation apparent in
her words. ''We could have loved him, Mother. We
could have provided him with everything. No one
would have questioned that.''

''Maybe,'' Pamela agreed, ''but…I would have resented him. I would have punished you and him. I
did punish you, darling, and I'm so very sorry.''

Trixie couldn't answer that. She'd longed to hear those very words from her mother for so long, yet the wounds were still too fresh, too raw, for her to accept them now. They'd all punished each other enough with this horrible deception, though.

"Too little, too late," Pamela said for her. "I know that now. I lost your father, and I had too much pride to come up to the ranch to try and win him back. So I became vindictive and bitter. And I used that bitterness against him when you got pregnant. I had the perfect weapon, the perfect opportunity to make him see that I'd been right all along."

Trixie held the album tight, then closed her weary eyes. "It's not all your fault. I was indiscreet and I was too ashamed, too confused, to own up to that indiscretion. But I should have fought harder to keep my child. I should have run away, back to Logan."

"We can go over and over this," Pamela said, her pragmatic side still burning strongly, "but facts are facts. We did what we had to do, to protect you and our name and our family. Maybe that seems shallow and self-serving now, but back then I suppose those were two of my main attributes."

Surprised, Trixie glanced up. "And now?"

"And now, I've had a lot of time to think about this. All it took was one look at that little boy's face." Pamela shifted, crossing her long legs and straightening her skirt, a daring look crossing her face. "And now, my darling, I am not ashamed anymore.

"So what if I have a grandson pop up out of the blue? Miriam Grisham has a daughter who's an alcoholic. She's having to raise her two teenaged granddaughters all by herself while their poor mother tries yet another rehab clinic. And I hear they're a real handful. I didn't turn away from Miriam at the country club, even though she tried to keep it hush-hush.

"And Reba Gallaway has a son who had to go to jail for shoplifting. She asked all of us to pray for him at church not two weeks ago. All of my friends have their own problems, in spite of their money and their big fancy houses. And I still consider them my friends—I worry about them, I feel for them and I do pray for them. I think I've just been praying in all the wrong ways, asking for the wrong things."

In spite of everything, Trixie couldn't help but laugh at her mother's misplaced logic. Comparing family crises at the country club! Now, there was a new one! Well, at least now Pamela was willing to admit there was a crisis in the Dunaway clan. And she was willing to do something about it. That willingness to let go of some of her iron-clad control and cold, firm denial endeared Pamela to Trixie in a way nothing else ever could.

"Oh, Mother, you are priceless," Trixie said now, some of the sadness leaving her for a brief moment.

Pamela held her head high, like a queen on a throne. "I have nothing to be ashamed of. I refuse to be ashamed of that beautiful child lying in that hospital bed. Besides, I'm getting too old and too impatient for all this pettiness. If my so-called friends can't support me in this, then pooh on them."

"Mother?"

Seeing the genuine surprise and shock on her daughter's face, Pamela shrugged, then turned serious. "It was like…like a light coming on. Seeing that little boy, realizing he was my own flesh and blood.

I was ashamed, all right. But not ashamed about what my friends might think. I became quite ashamed of myself. I tried to deny one of my own.'' Sitting up to pat her hair, she added, ''Dunaways do not turn family away. We stick together. And it's high time I remember that.''

Trixie handed the album to her mother. ''I wish Daddy could hear you saying that. He'd be so proud.''

''Me, too,'' Pamela admitted. ''You know, I miss your father so much. We could have grown old together, only I was too full of pride to forgive him, or to ask him to forgive me.''

''I think he knows,'' Trixie said. ''I think he always knew that you loved him in your heart.''

''I hope so,'' Pamela replied. Her eyes settling on her daughter's, she added, ''Do you know, Logan told me that Brant talked about me the day he died?''

Amazed that Logan and her mother had even had a civil conversation, Trixie said, ''Really?''

''Really. He said Brant told him that he missed his Pammy. And that he loved me.''

''That's so sweet, Mother. You have to remember that.''

''I will, always.'' Looking down at the scrapbook, she said, ''Now, what's this?''

''Pictures of your grandson,'' Trixie told her. ''And, there's some of Daddy, too.''

''Oh,'' Pamela said, her eyes widening, tears springing up in their depths. ''Oh, that Brant. He always was a big ham.''

''Our big lovable ham,'' Trixie replied. ''Look at

the pictures, Mother. And while you're looking, try to forgive yourself.''

Pamela nodded. ''I will if you will.''

Trixie stood up, the little bit of laughter her talk with her mother had inadvertently provided gone now as the solemn weight of her son's accident hit her squarely on the shoulders. She turned to give her mother a parting glance. ''I'll forgive myself when my son is safe and well.''

Worried, Pamela stood up to follow her. ''Trixie, don't blame yourself for this, sugar. It was an accident.''

''Was it, Mother? I wonder. Was it an accident, or was it meant to happen exactly this way?''

Appalled, Pamela hurried after her daughter. ''No, darling. You can't think like that. We have to keep the faith and hold fast.''

Trixie bobbed her head then. ''I'll hold fast—to my son. And this time, I won't let him go.''

''She blames herself,'' Harlan told Logan the next afternoon as they sat in the waiting room.

The doctor had given Trixie, Logan and Harlan a full report, and Trixie had rushed back into Caleb's room, visibly upset.

''Five days in a coma, and no response. That is cause for concern, but we're still optimistic,'' Dr. Arnold had said to them in his monotone way a few minutes earlier.

''Doctors,'' Logan said, worry causing him to lash out at the very ones who'd helped keep his son alive. ''They talk in such riddles.''

''They're doing everything they can, son,'' Harlan

assured him. "But I still say we can move him to Houston. I'll round up a passle of the best specialists money can buy."

Logan appreciated Harlan's offer, but resented the power of his money. "You've already brought in a specialist from Little Rock," he reminded Harlan. "And he told us the same thing as Dr. Arnold. They've done everything they can. Now we just have to wait and hope."

"And pray," Harlan reminded him. "Some things even my money can't buy."

Logan wondered if he'd been asking God for the wrong things himself. He only wanted God to save his son, but maybe it was time to accept that he had no control over that. Maybe it was time to just turn it all over to the Lord and accept whatever happened. That wouldn't be easy, but he was running out of options.

"I'm going in to see him," he told Harlan as he pushed up off one of the many comfortable chairs provided in the waiting area.

He found Trixie in her familiar spot, sitting by her son's bed, her hand intertwined with Caleb's, her face drawn and desperate, her voice pleading and firm at the same time.

"Get well, honey. We all miss you so much. Please, Caleb, open your eyes and talk to me."

Logan came to stand by her side. He was worried about her; she hadn't left the hospital in over twenty-four hours. First her father's death and now this. No one could stand up to that much stress for very long.

"Tricia Maria," he said, his voice low and coaxing, "why don't we go back out to the ranch for a while. You can get some sleep, and I'll make you some of my famous chili.''

''No.'' She didn't look at him. Her eyes remained on her child. ''I'm not tired.''

Logan knew what she was trying to do. She was pouring seven years of lost time into what might be her last hours with her son. ''Trixie, honey, you're making yourself sick. You can't keep up this pace.''

Turning to him at last, Trixie stared hard into his eyes, tiredness making her edgy with resentment. ''I refuse to leave him,'' she said, a frown marring her face. ''I left him once. I promised him I won't do it again.''

She was stubborn, that was for sure. And still angry.

''He knows you love him, Trixie. He has to know that.''

''Does he? How can he, Logan, when he never even knew I existed?''

He didn't miss the accusation in her words. They'd all reached the end of their ropes and tension was bound to make them say things they'd regret later. Taking a minute to calm himself, he tried to reason with her again. ''Listen, honey, it was wrong of me not to tell you about him, but we've been through all of that.''

Hating herself for her harsh words, Trixie looked back down at her son, wishing with all of her heart she could just let go and turn things over to God. But she still had too much fight left in her. She wasn't quite ready to relinquish control.

Her voice soft now, she said, ''When were you planning on telling me about him, Logan? If my father hadn't died, would I have ever known about my son?''

A valid question. A hard question to answer. But she needed answers, and she'd hit on one of the things that had been eating at him the most.

''I honestly don't know,'' he admitted as he came to stand by her. ''When you came back to the ranch, I was so afraid you'd find out. So we tried to protect him from you.''

She gave him a quick glance, then returned her concentration to Caleb, her eyes darting here and there over her son's face. ''That much I've figured out. You must have really wrestled with that one. If I sold the ranch, you could possibly be booted off the place, but if I kept the ranch, you risked my finding out the truth.''

''Yes, and I'm not proud of it…or the way I treated you.''

She lifted her eyes to his, slamming him with a look of anguish and hurt. ''How long would this have gone on?''

Logan lowered his head, the guilt of his deception coloring his face. ''I don't know. But I do know that one thought has been uppermost in my mind since the accident.''

Trixie heard the regret in his voice. Immediately she felt remorse for her angry, accusing words. ''Oh, Logan. I'm sorry. You're right, I am so very tired. And trying to lay blame won't help Caleb now.''

Logan knelt, them placed his hand on top of hers over Caleb's. ''If it's any consolation, I had planned on telling you everything that night at dinner, the night of the storm.''

"The night of Caleb's accident," she said, awe filling her words. "Isn't life ironic? I was going to tell you that night that I'd given your child up. I figured we could never be happy together with such a horrible secret between us."

"I felt the same way," he said, his eyes holding hers. "I only knew we had to forgive, before we could ever forget and move on with things. Do you think we can ever get over this, Trixie?"

She looked down at their hands. Logan's big hand covered hers, while her fingers held on to Caleb's smaller hand. It seemed so bittersweet that they were together now. But they were, and that gave her a small measure of hope.

She watched Logan, hoping he'd see the love in her heart. "Think about it. We were willing to risk losing each other again, by telling the truth at last. That has to count for something."

Logan grinned then, relief washing over him. "You're so smart."

"Not smart," she said. "Just tired of fighting against my heart." She pressed her lips to his jawline, then sat back. "I do love you, Logan. That is the real truth. And I know we've got a lot to work through. If…if Caleb doesn't make it, I don't know if we can, either."

Logan understood what she was saying. The pain would be too great, the loss too overwhelming, for them to ever find happiness together again. Suddenly he knew what they had to do.

"Trixie, listen to me," he said, his voice low and full of pain. "We've been praying for the wrong things. We've asked God to spare our child, but it's not up to us to ask that."

Shocked, she raised her eyebrows. "Well, I intend to keep on asking, whether it's my place or not."

"Hear me out," he said, his hand on hers tightening. "Maybe we should just turn it all over to God. Maybe instead of blaming each other, and rehashing all the old hurts, we should just let go and give this burden to the Lord."

"Just give up?"

"No, honey. We won't be giving up. We'll be letting go—of all the pain, all the sins and the lies, all the bitterness. Maybe that's the only real way we can help our son."

Tears pricked her eyes. "Now look who's so smart."

Logan shook his head. "No, actually I've been a fool. We know we love each other, but we forgot one important element of love."

"What's that?"

"Trust," he replied, his gaze slipping from her to his son. "We forgot to put our trust in each other, and in the Lord."

He was right. All of these many years, she'd believed she was in total control, while all along she'd let others control her life. Pamela. Harlan. Radford. Never once had she turned things over to God, not in the real sense of the word. And she'd never really trusted anyone, because all of those around her had let her down so many times.

Except God.

Somehow He'd brought her back here to be with

her son. Somehow, through all of the pain, He'd shown her the truth.

"Okay," she said, "I'm willing, Lord. I'm turning this burden over to You. I leave my son in Your hands. And whether he lives or dies, I trust You to protect him and watch over him."

"Me, too, Lord," Logan echoed.

They both let go of Caleb's hand, then turned to each other, a new hope, a new peace apparent in their expressions as they held each other close.

"I love you," Logan said.

"I love you, too." Trixie held tight to that, even as she gave up control. Then she whispered, "And I trust you—completely."

"Enough to eat my chili?" he asked, his eyes bright with tears and laughter.

"Yes," she answered, laughing. "Even that much. But another time. I'm not leaving the hospital."

"Still stubborn," Logan whispered. But he took her hand, and together they sat, watching over their son.

Much later, Gayle came back in, ready to take over the constant vigil.

"Your mother and I had a long talk," she informed Trixie, her tone as firm and unyielding as ever. "I think we've reached an understanding."

"I'm glad, I think," Trixie said, wondering just what kind of understanding these two very different women had reached.

Trying to reassure her, Gayle smiled. "Your mother is a very strong woman. I admire that much about her. I think I can tolerate her, after all."

"Another miracle," Logan whispered.

Chapter Fifteen

Gayle sat huddled near her grandson's bed, her hand in his. Logan stood in the corner, his eyes never leaving his son's face. Trixie watched from outside, through the glass window to her son's room. She'd sent Pamela back to the ranch earlier to get her a suitcase of fresh clothes. They were all afraid to leave the hospital now.

Caleb wasn't responding to any of the treatment the medical staff had tried. As the minutes turned into hours, Trixie's heart began to sink once again. She had to accept that Caleb might not ever wake up.

And still she prayed. Still she held out hope as she gazed at her child. So small. So very innocent.

How should she ask God for help?

Should she promise to walk away, if only He'd spare her child? Should she beg, plead, bargain, barter, threaten, or should she simply get down on her knees and hand it all over to Him?

"I'm so tired, Lord," she said, her eyes on Logan.

"So tired. I can't bear this alone. I've fought against this for so long, holding my sin in my heart. And now, the truth has come out. Don't make my son suffer anymore. That's all I ask. And please, help me to forgive and to understand why they kept my child from me. And help Logan to heal, too. Help me, help us, Lord.''

She turned away from the window, unable to watch Logan's tortured face any longer. Harlan was there, with outstretched arms. Trixie willingly ran to him, letting him tug her close in the comfort and security of his arms. "Granddaddy, I don't think I'll make it if he dies.''

"Hang in there, honey,'' Harlan said, his tone sweet and encouraging. "It ain't over till it's over. As long as there's breath in him, there's still hope.''

"But will it ever really be over?'' she asked as he guided her to a chair. "I mean, if Caleb does make it, we still have so many problems to deal with. Logan and I held our secrets so well—how can we learn to really trust each other again?''

"Love,'' her grandfather replied simply. "Love, darling. That's the miracle.''

"I don't think there are any miracles left,'' she said, laying her head on his shoulder.

"You rest, then,'' he replied, his big hand patting her arm. "And leave the miracles up to the man in charge.''

Logan came out into the hallway, his gaze scanning the area until his eyes settled on Trixie. "Can we talk?''

Harlan rose out of his seat, then glanced down at his granddaughter. "Do you want me to stay?''

"No. I'll be okay."

"Then, I'll go in and see my great-grandson," he said as he shot Logan a worried glance.

Somewhere across the way, a television set blared the evening news. A car commercial came on, the pitch man spouting out the deal of a lifetime. Logan glared at the television as if it were the cause of all of his problems.

"What is it?" Trixie asked, bracing herself for the worst.

He took her hand, his eyes gentle. "I just wanted—"

But Trixie's gaze was fixed on the television now. "Logan, look. It's my mother."

Pamela stood on the back porch of the ranch house, her tasteful jewelry glittering in the late afternoon sun. "And I'd just like to clarify the entire situation. I repeat, Mr. Logan Maxwell, foreman of Brant Dunaway Farms International, has in no way jeopardized or neglected any of the children in his care. In fact, a social worker just finished investigating these unjustified allegations and I believe her report will indicate that the rumors regarding this ranch are unfounded and clearly false."

"What?" Logan glared at the television, in shock. "What is she talking about?"

Trixie could only shake her head. "I have no idea."

The camera moved to another woman standing with Pamela.

Logan groaned. "That's Mrs. Wilder, the social worker for the ranch. She comes by periodically to check on things and make sure the children are okay. But what's she doing with your mother?''

''Mrs. Dunaway is correct on all counts,'' the young woman said, her stance confident. ''I've interviewed all of the children here, as well as the counselors and volunteers, and I feel confident that these allegations are totally false. Mr. Maxwell hasn't been neglecting his duties here. He's been at the county hospital with his son. The boy was involved in a four-wheeler accident.''

Trixie looked over at Logan, her mouth open in amazement. ''Rad,'' she said, realization sweeping through her. ''He threatened to make trouble, and apparently he did just that.''

Logan shook his head. ''I'd better head out there to see what this is all about.''

''Wait,'' Trixie said. ''Knowing my mother, that might not be necessary.''

When the camera panned back to her mother, Pamela beamed. ''Of course, Ms. Wilder is just doing her job based on the unsubstantiated rumors she's heard, but I can assure the good citizens of Arkansas that the Brant Dunaway Ranch is a strong, viable refuge for troubled teens and other children with special needs. My family has contributed largely to this project, and we have always been completely satisfied and pleased with the work here. Logan Maxwell is a good man, and a hardworking, highly trained individual. And I, along with several of the best attorneys in the state, dare anyone to prove otherwise.''

''She's obviously delusional,'' Logan said, the black humor breaking some of the tension he'd felt all morning. "I mean, since when does your mother go around defending me?"

Trixie looked into his eyes. "I'm sure we'll hear all the details later. But I believe my mother just stood up for you because she realized that you are a good and decent man, and that I love you."

"How?" he asked, the awe in the one word causing him to hang his head.

"How what?" Trixie lifted his chin with a finger. "How can she defend you? How can I love you?"

"That about sums it up," he said, his hands settling on her shoulders. "I've been such a—"

"You've been worried about your son and the ranch," she interjected. "And I've been holding back."

"Another secret?" he asked, forgetting the drama unfolding on the evening news.

Trixie took his hand. "Not really a secret. Just a little bit of resentment. I resented you for keeping Caleb away from me. But I know in my heart, I wouldn't have wanted him to be raised by anyone else. You are his father, after all."

He looked away, down at the floor. "But it was cruel to keep him from you. You have to know how I feel."

"I do," she said, her hand moving over his face. "I know that we love each other, and Granddaddy says that's all we need. But, Logan, we have a lot to work through. I don't even know if I'll ever be able to tell Caleb the truth."

"Your granddaddy's right," Logan replied, his own hands coming up to touch her face. "Our love has to be strong, Trixie. We'll do it right this time—

we'll get married. We'll take it a step at a time. And the first step is to hold tight to each other, while we pray for our son. Nothing else matters right now—not even the ranch.''

She nodded her agreement. ''With my mother in charge, I can assure you the ranch is in good hands, no matter what Rad or anyone else tries to pull.''

Logan managed a weak grin. ''There's a scary thought.''

''Trust me,'' Trixie reminded him. ''If Rad did try to stir up trouble, my mother would set him straight good and proper.''

Logan tugged her into his arms, then closing his eyes in a silent, gentle prayer, all of the anger leaving him as he leaned on the strength of her love.

Trixie held to him, letting him anchor her there, letting him tell her with his touch and his kiss that he would always forgive her, no matter what.

They would fight, together, for the ranch, for their child, for their love. And with God's help, they'd survive.

A commotion all around them brought them out of their embrace.

''The doctors,'' Logan managed to shout, his face going pale. ''They're headed into Caleb's room.''

''I called them,'' Gayle replied from behind them. ''Oh, Logan, he's awake. Caleb's awake.''

Tears of gratitude and joy fell down Trixie's face as she followed Logan into the room, their hands held tightly together while several doctors hurried to examine their son.

''Daddy?'' Caleb called, his voice weak, his eyes widening at the sight of his father.

"I'm here, pal," Logan said, moving to the bed as doctors rushed past him to check all of Caleb's vital signs. "How ya doing?"

"Okay, I guess. Where's my hat?"

Trixie stood there with Logan, laughing and crying at the same time. "It's right here," she managed to say as she held up the battered cowboy hat.

"What happened?" Caleb asked, his little boy eyes bright with a million questions.

Logan looked from his son to Trixie, heaving a sigh of relief. "That, son, is a long story."

"Okay," Caleb said, drowsy again. "Hey, Miss Trixie, when we get home, will you finally, finally come and see my kittens?"

Trixie leaned close to place a kiss on her son's forehead as she reaped the joy of a new beginning. "I sure will. I love stray kittens."

Epilogue

One year later

"Come on, sport," Logan called to his son. "We got a new crop of volunteers to break in."

Trixie and Caleb both came down the porch steps, laughing and giggling as the morning sun lifted its shy head over the eastern horizon. Samantha followed close behind, her grin as wide as the sun.

"You two behave now," Logan warned his wife and son. "Don't want to scare them off before they even get to enjoy pig duty."

Caleb stepped up by his father, taking Logan's hand in his own. Then he turned to Trixie, reaching out a hand to her as several people piled out of trucks and cars, eager to spend a few days helping on the ranch.

"Hey, folks," he said before Logan could utter a word. Pulling Trixie and Logan forward, the little boy grinned. "This is my daddy, Logan." Then he looked up at Trixie, his eyes as vivid and blue as the autumn sky. "And this is my mama, Tricia Maria. You can call her Trixie."

Everyone laughed as Trixie bent down to hug her son close. "And you, silly boy, can go in and finish your breakfast."

Caleb giggled and ran toward the house where Gayle waved, then Samantha took charge with the new volunteers, leaving the little boy's parents to gaze into each other's eyes. It had been a tough year, full of struggles and changes, but they had made it through.

Pamela had headed Rad's accusations off at the pass that day on the steps of the ranch house. She and the formidable Mrs. Wilder were now the best of friends. And Pamela was one of the most visible patrons of The Brant Dunaway International Farms. Her work here had brought Trixie's mother a certain amount of fame in both Texas and Arkansas. Pamela, in true socialite fashion, was having the time of her life. And so was her daughter.

Trixie smiled over at her husband, then patted the baby just beginning to grow inside her stomach. Soon they'd be in their new home, near the sunflowers, near the mountains.

"It's going to be a wonderful harvest, Mr. Maxwell," she said, all the love in her heart shining in her eyes.

Logan touched a hand to her stomach. "Every day's wonderful with you and Caleb here," he said. "And our little Harlan Branton Maxwell in there."

"What if it's a Pamela Gayle Maxwell instead?"

Logan rolled his eyes skyward. "Perish the thought."

Trixie snuggled close, kissing his jaw. "You know you love both of them."

"I know I love you," he replied. Then he kissed her. "Now, let's get to work."

"I'm ready," Trixie replied, her eyes scanning the distant mountains as she thanked God for blessing her with this second chance. Then she remembered one other very important person who would always hold a special place in her heart. "Thanks, Daddy."

The warm September wind lifted her hair away from her face, and one perfect golden leaf glided down from the great oak standing in the yard. Trixie caught it, smiled, then let it go, her heart filled with love.

And at long last, joy.

* * * * *

Dear Reader,

This book is all about second chances. Sometimes we make decisions that will ultimately change our lives forever. And sometimes we regret the choices we are forced to make. There are people out there who suffer each and every day for choices they made long ago. But I believe hope springs eternal. We might not be able to go back and change the past, but with God's help, we can move forward to the future. We have to look for the joy, and when we do get an opportunity to make things right, we have to take it and know that God is watching over us always.

This book was a joy to write because I've actually been on a ranch similar to the one in this book. That's where I got to know Cindy, who has turned out to be one of my closest and dearest friends. We had pig duty and yes, we did meet "The Pigmeister" himself, a handsome, intense young man who was determined to show the volunteers from the big city what ranch life was all about. After a massive attack of allergies, we survived and still laugh about our adventures today.

We found the joy of friendship.

Hope you find yours, too.

Until next time, may the angels watch over you while you sleep.

Lenora Worth

Concluding in May from

VOWS

a series by
Irene Hannon

Don't miss the conclusion to this deeply emotional
series about three close friends....

*Each has a secret hidden in their past.
Each will experience the love of their own special
man. But will they be able to conquer the shadows
which still plague them...and look to the
future with renewed faith?*

The series began in October with...
HOME FOR THE HOLIDAYS

Continued in February with...
A GROOM OF HER OWN

And concludes in May with...
A FAMILY TO CALL HER OWN

When Rebecca Matthews fell for dashing Zach Wright,
he offered her a glimpse of happily-ever-after.
However, a traumatic incident in her past warned her
not to dream of a family of her own. But then Zach
became the guardian of a precious little girl, and
Rebecca knew the Lord wouldn't want to turn away
from this man and child....

Only from *Love Inspired.*

Take 3 inspirational love stories FREE!

PLUS get a FREE surprise gift!

Special Limited-time Offer

**Mail to Steeple Hill Reader Service™
3010 Walden Avenue
P.O. Box 1867
Buffalo, N.Y. 14240-1867**

YES! Please send me 3 free Love Inspired™ novels and my free surprise gift. Then send me 3 brand-new novels every month, which I will receive months before they appear in bookstores. Bill me at the low price of $3.19 each plus 25¢ delivery and applicable sales tax, if any*. That's the complete price and a saving of over 10% off the cover prices—quite a bargain! I understand that accepting the books and gift places me under no obligation ever to buy any books. I can always return a shipment and cancel at any time. Even if I never buy another book from Steeple Hill, the 3 free books and the surprise gift are mine to keep forever.

103 IEN CFAG

Name	(PLEASE PRINT)	
Address		Apt. No.
City	State	Zip